THE NEXT PROJECT

R. C. STITH

Atomic Alien Publishing

Note: All characters and events in the story are not based on any actual events and are completely fictional.

THE NEXT PROJECT

Copyright © 2005, 2008 by Ryan C. Stith

ISBN 978-0-6151-6899-9

Printed in the United States of America
Atomic Alien Publishing
Third edition / January 2008

Atomic Alien Publishing is a registered sub brand of Atomic Alien Productions.
For more information visit, www.atomicalien.s5.com.

FATHER OF DARKNESS

THE
NEXT
PROJECT

Volume 1

VISIT www.atomicalien.s5.com FOR MORE

ON THE FATHER OF DARKNESS SERIES.

COMING ON 08 / 08 / 08

More of "Father Of Darkness" Series,

The Next Project Volume 2

AND

Followers of Julian

Also by Ryan C. Stith

DEAD COLD REVENGE

Coming early 2009

Atomic Alien Publishing contact

(407) 459-4636

http://www.atomicalien.s5.com

Ryan C. Stith

To the loved ones I've lost --
You are all on my mind and in my heart.

PROLOGUE

"The view from the top is always worth the climb."

A blood chilling cry rang out in the darkness of the mammoth cave like structure. Water steadily dripped into a puddle next to a whining adolescent dinosaur. Frightened and all alone in the corner the tiny creature moved out of the darkness while crying out for its provider. Outside asteroids rocketed through the atmosphere screaming past thousands of charging dinosaurs.

The adolescent dinosaur emerged from the moss covered cave and raised its head to the sky. The Sun was blood red and blinding white light pierced all the space around them. The most primitive of creatures had realized its inherent doom. Immense orbs of melting, fire charged rock, as bright as ten suns glided into the atmosphere and plowed into the devastated planet. Herds of dinosaurs from all species charged across the burning plains together from the inescapable wrath of their inevitable fate.

Even brighter flashes suddenly overpowered the incoming fireballs. The flashes of white light somehow skewed reality for the moment, almost like static interfering with a television broadcast. Strange unrelated images appeared in the sky, many were too blurry to make out other than a symbol that resembled a Celtic cross. Another looked like a human figure shadowed by a glowing gold halo.

The dinosaurs existence had been abandoned. The herd of remaining dinosaur charged across the burning hillside as an image appeared in the sky of hundreds of humans gathered upon a hilltop looking to the heavens.

God is within us all.

Another enormous asteroid was rocketing toward Earth. The burning rock melted and lost mass as boiling magma burned up rapidly through the atmosphere. More and more asteroids shot across the sky and collided with the planet, devastating the entire herd of dinosaurs. The helpless creatures were eradicated dozens at a time. Soon, the largest asteroid hundreds of meters in diameter impacted directly into the cave structure causing catastrophic results.

There was one last flash of white light.

Malivick Devoe jumped up from his bed.

It was just a dream.

Malivick's face glistened in the moon-light as he laid back and tried to get comfortable in his king bed. Malivick drifted deeply in his mind for a few minutes before looking at his digital clock and curling back up in bed to keep warm.

CHAPTER ONE

"Blood is Thicker Than Water"

```
"Great is the art of beginning, but greater is the art
                    of ending."
                  - Lazarus Long
```

Denver, Colorado – December 2012

Thousands of college football fans jammed the Denver coliseum. Many of them came to see not only the rivalry of two teams, but also twin brothers who had captured the attention of the nation with their agility, power and courageous athleticism.

THE NEXT PROJECT

The University of Colorado's offense breaks from the huddle and headed to the line led by Malivick Devoe, the Falcon's star Quarterback. The brand new stadium was at capacity on that particularly hot autumn day. It registered at 120 degrees Fahrenheit. That set a new record high for December, which had become commonplace the last several years. Global warming had done a real number on the planet, especially three years ago when an enormous amount of polar ice caps melted in the warmer waters, causing much of Florida and Louisiana to be completely submerged permanently. Many other low lying areas around the world suffered catastrophic losses as well. Most thought it was the beginning of the end, but humans have persisted to not live in fear and continue the way of life they have come to know and love.

Inside the stadium deafening cheers drowned the enthusiasm of the announcer.

Malivick stepped up in the shot-gun formation, his eyes hidden behind a mirrored visor. The snap initiated a brutal clash of the teams colors, both red and white. Malivick dropped back as a middle linebacker clawed his way into the backfield headed for the Quarterback.

"Fraizer over the center, all over Malivick. But No!" The Announcer yelled excitedly.

Malivick ducked low and Jonny Fraizer in mid air sailed clean over his head. He scrambled out of the pocket, and looked for his main receiver, but he was still being covered by number eighty.

"Looking to throw. Cyrus is closing in. And he has nothing open. Vik rolls back out to the left side under heavy pressure!" The announcer shouted amazed by the commitment demonstrated on the field.

Malivick dodged two more attempts at a tackle; his brother Cyrus Devoe dropped back over to cover the second receiver! Malivick pump faked then threw a laser of a pass down the field. His receiver, Clayton Mills number eighty-eight, was a tall leggy possession receiver. He jumped high in the air to make the catch, but Cyrus Devoe hit him hard in mid air and the football popped loose and hit the ground. "Incomplete pass!" The announcer interjected, "These are two of the best football players in the nation and I would say in the very near future, they will be known as the best in the world."

"Too slow man!" Malivick taunted his opponent, then jogged back to the huddle.

"Alright, Flood right 32 outs jag z." Malivick watched the sideline for the next play. His leadership skills were profoundly effective not only on teammates and friends, but to all who he came in contact with.

"Randall Fisher is checking in for Malivick. But why?" The announcer's disembodied voice exclaimed in awkward astonishment. He couldn't understand what would warrant such a move. "What is Coach Bly thinking? He will be the number one draft pick in the World League for next season!"

THE NEXT PROJECT

The Colorado State Falcons backup Quarterback, Randall Fischer jogged to the huddle with a look of discontent and heart-break. Randall couldn't bare to look Malivick in the eyes. He could only stare down at the white chalk lines on the field. "Vik, you're out," Fischer told him. "Coach needs to talk to you."

"What!?" Malivick couldn't believe it and he didn't even attempt to understand.

"Just go. Vik, just go." Randall interrupted him and took over the huddle. Randall watched as Malivick paced back to the sideline and was received by a chorus of boos from the unhappy fans. His twin brother Cyrus also watched on in confusion.

"This is unheard of!" The announcer roared louder than before.

Inside the defensive huddle Cyrus kept his focus on Malivick intently.

Something isn't right.

"BREAK!" The defense broke from the huddle and trotted to the line of scrimmage. On the home team sideline, Malivick removed his helmet and faced his Head Coach Michael Bly.

The play started but Cyrus was determined to see what was happening with his brother while at the same time keeping his head in the game. He was able to focus on the ball carrier and was on the tackle of the halfback. The rusher was number thirty-two, Clint Barnes. A long time friend of Malivick and the family. Cyrus got up from the pile and looked up and down the sideline for his brother.

Cyrus could hear his head coach calling his name, but he was intently searching for Malivick. "CYRUS, OFF THE FIELD!"

Coach Andale shouted. He jotted on the field to get Cyrus' attention.

Once again the crowd roared in disbelief. Cyrus finally gave in and went to the sideline.

"Cyrus..." Coach Andale said.

Spit it out.

"Something happened to you're father." Coach added.

"What happened? Where is he?", Cyrus panicked immediately.

"Maybe we should go to the back and talk about this." Coach Andale said in an attempt to calm Cyrus down.

"Malivick Devoe has left the stadium." The announcers words burned a hole straight through Cyrus' expression.

I have to get out of here.

CHAPTER TWO

"Going Home"

"Let us not look back in anger or forward in fear, but
around in awareness."
- James Thurber

The warm desert wind kicked up and whipped over a remarkable sunset on the horizon as a small gleam in the sky moved into view.

Inside the commercial Boeing Jet, the flight attendants roamed the isles and catered to the needs of the crass and uptight first class passengers.

Malivick and Cyrus occupied the third row back from the cockpit next to the window. Both of them sat quietly. Cyrus's messy black hair was styled with streaks to accent his dark complexion, and his athletic stature suited him well. He had a calmness about him not unusual to his mentality of remaining tranquil during stressful situations. Cyrus was always in control.

His brother Malivick had longer jet black hair styled a bit differently. He also remained calm and collected in strenuous circumstances. Malivick was physically bigger and stronger than Cyrus, and his eyes were as deep and blue as the ocean, and always focused on his top priority.

I hate this awkward silence.

"Vik, I know we haven't had much time to think about all of this, but I have to tell you about this feeling I had," Cyrus hesitated. "It's like something inside tells me that something bad is about to happen, and..." Cyrus leaned closer to his brother, so that only he could hear. "I don't mean about Dad. Something more, something... I can't explain."

Malivick nodded as if he understood fully what his brother was going through. "You don't have to explain it Cyrus." Malivick said. "I had the same feeling. Like a sign or a message, but I have to believe it was the will of God to show us that it was the right thing to come home. For Dad's sake."

Cyrus thinks so too. He just needed reassurance from his balance. "It was the right thing to do. *Wasn't it?*"

Malivick sat up straight in his seat, somewhat frustrated by what his brother said. "Family comes first, no matter how big of a game.

Dad taught us that and we owe him that, and more," Malivick added. "Why would you even question that?"

Cyrus wasn't sure what to say. He kept his composure and plead his case. "All I am saying is that this game was going to decide our career. Our last game before the draft."

Do I need to say more?

Cyrus for the first time felt disconnected from his ordinarily grounded equal. "Now, we both know we can be unstoppable, but since we left the game, will we even get our chance to prove ourselves in the World League?" Cyrus extinguished his thoughts.

"We will make them hear us." Malivick said. "We just need to take this time to go home and catch up." Malivick's inherited patience and wisdom helped him handle his brother.

In the passenger panel above every seat on the plane a light blinked on instructing everyone to fasten their seat belts. Moments later the co-pilot appeared on the projection screen in first class and on the display screens embedded inside the back of each seat. He spoke calmly and instructed the passengers of the arrival procedures upon landing. Cyrus was lost in his mind.

It will be good to be back home...

The cabin pressure suddenly decreased dramatically during decent and the oxygen masks dropped down in front of all the passengers. Many people shouted in panic. The Co-pilot blamed turbulence for the dramatic change in altitude and cabin pressure. He ensured that the turbulence would be gone momentarily and that there was nothing to worry about.

The jet suddenly dropped again slightly and began to shake even more violently. Malivick didn't seem to be worried.

Cyrus glanced at Malivick as a look of unconscious pain came over his face. His limbs flailed around uncontrollably as his eyes grew lifeless. Cyrus unbuckled his seat belt and turned to help his brother. "Malivick! Wake up!" Cyrus yelled franticly. He jumped out of his seat and down the aisle to the attendant seating station. He brought back two female flight attendants and the older of the two checked Malivick's pulse. Just as Cyrus turned around to his brother, the jet dropped forward uncontrollably.

Cyrus stumbled forward, lost his balance, and sailed head over heals down the aisle.

He flipped in mid air before crashing to a stop on the cockpit containment door, hard. Many frightened passengers cried and screamed to their loved ones. In the cockpit the pilot pulled up to stabilize the jet. The reverse thrusters kicked in and caused the plane to rumble forward. The turbulence ceased just moments before the nose of the plane touched down. The passengers realized they were finally safe. The attendant rushed to check on Cyrus, the other tended to Malivick. They were both unconscious.

"Give us some room!" The attendant shouted. She was just about to perform CPR on Cyrus, when a gray haired man two rows behind where the brothers were seated comes forward.

"I'm a doctor. Let me through." He knelt beside Cyrus and checked his vital signs. "Don't move him. He might have broken his neck." The doctor moves to the other sibling still belted into his seat restraint. Malivick is slouched down in his seat, his head slumped to the side. "This is very strange. He seems to be fine. Heart rate is normal. No signs of trauma." The doctor was confused. He reached inside Cyrus' back pocket and pulled out his wallet. He looked inside and removed his drivers license. He handed the wallet and the ID to the attendant. "I think you should contact their family. Find out if they have any family illnesses." The doctor stood to his feet as the plane door opened and paramedics rush in to aid the fallen brothers from the jetway.

CHAPTER THREE

"Seven Days Later"

"Time does not change us.
It just unfolds us."
- Max Frisch

It was a cloudy night in mid city unknown. Rain poured down the sides of the modern skyscrapers, flowed through the streets, and into a drain in front of the emergency room entrance. A slew of cars circled the bustling parking lot on this unusually busy night.

Two emergency medical service workers emerge through the automatic doors in heavy coats and scarfs around their face ready to battle the wet and windy conditions. They climbed into the cab of an ambulance and as the ambulance pulled away from the emergency room drop off, the flashing emergency signals extinguished and the emergency response vehicle disappeared into the night.

Inside the main building of the hospital, on the third floor, a chart labeled, 'DEVOE, CYRUS – TRAUMA' hung from the door numbered 607.

"My boys have been in intensive care, unconscious for seven days and you still can't tell me what is wrong with them?" A saddened and tearful female voice chimed from inside the room.

Room 607, like the others, had a dry and generically sterile appearance. The smell of ammonia lingered throughout the trauma unit. The room was plain as could be with only the hospital bed, Cyrus' monitoring equipment and a single chair. A white patternless curtain surrounded half of Cyrus' bed and covered another bare white wall. It would have been a grand place for a window. The voice of the woman who spoke held firm on her sons hand as he laid in a comatose state. Cyrus resembled his mother in complexion and similar facial features. Her fear and angst were fluently exhibited through the wrinkles on her aged face. "I thought this was a hospital. Isn't that what you do? Diagnose and heal!" Misses Devoe almost broke down.

Doctor Rayburn, a tall and slender, tell it like it is man, stood in front of Misses Devoe. "Listen, Cyrus has a bad bruise on his head and shoulder," The doctor's expression changed to bewilderment as he sat next to the bed and looked over at Cyrus in his sleep. "But that is no reason for what has happened to him." He paused a moment. "And Malivick - not a scratch. He is in outstanding physical condition. It doesn't make any sense."

A single tear rolled down her face. The kind doctor handed her a tissue that he pulled from his coat pocket. "There must be something more to this," He continued. "And I assure you that we will get to the bottom of it. We are running other tests on Malivick now to see what more we can find." The doctor turned and walked mother to the door. "I know you must be extremely worried, but I suggest that you get some fresh air." He told her. "You haven't left the room for five days."

Misses Devoe's contorted face finally straightened as she looked up at Doctor Rayburn.

Has it really been that long?

Doctor Rayburn led her out of the room and down the hospital hallway. They passed two nurses as they walked through the narrow corridor.

"Doctor, I'm sorry about what I said." Misses Devoe offered. "It's just, a week ago I lost my husband, today I could lose my sons, and I believe if that happens then tomorrow it could easily be me." Mother lowered her head and began to cry to herself. Doctor Rayburn placed a hand on Misses Devoes' back in an effort to comfort her.

"Don't say things like that," The doctor said. "Things *will* get better." He tried his best to console her even though he was used to dealing with death on a daily basis.

"Better?" Misses Devoe didn't understand. "How?" Doctor Rayburn had no good answer. "Are you going to bring my husband back doctor?" She shot back rhetorically. Before Rayburn could say a word, the doctor's pager beeped. He unclipped it from his coat pocket and squinted at the tiny lettering.

"I'm sorry Misses Devoe, I will be back to check on Cyrus soon. I promise."

The doctor ran off as Mother stepped out back onto the hospital lawn.

Lightning struck and thunder rolled through the heavens as rain sprinkled upon her knotted hair and ran down her face. Her appearance was evidence she had been not seen a mirror in some time. She began to cry but held back her tears. She dabbed the rain from her face with the tissue the doctor had given her, when suddenly her expression shifted to severe distress. Maybe it was maternal instincts.

Something isn't right.

Mother rushed back down the long hallway, and back into Cyrus' room. She pulled back the curtain that hid the bed.

"My son! Where is my son?!" Mother shouted. She grabbed the closest nurse who was two doors down. She was already hysterical, screaming as she ran through the halls.

The nurse tried to calm the panic stricken mother. "Malivick is in testing, remember Misses Devoe?" The nurse offered.

"NO! Not Malivick, Where is Cyrus?!?" Misses Devoe demanded.

"You mean he's not in his bed?" The nurse was now concerned. They both hurried back to room 607, just as another doctor entered.

"What is going on here?" the doctor asked. The nurse could not believe it. "Doctor, the patient is missing!" the nurse told him. "I don't understand. No one came out!"

"Missing?" The doctor asked as his pager beeped. He looked at the page and was immediately horrified. Misses Devoe had a feeling it wasn't good.

"What is it!?" Misses Devoe yelled.

"Malivick is missing out of testing," the doctor told her. "I don't know how this could happen..."

CHAPTER FOUR

"A Shocking Discovery"

"How use doth breed a habit in man."
- William Shakespeare

The full moon loomed brightly between the tallest buildings of a run-down and nearly deserted city district. Dogs howled at sirens that echoed somewhere in the distance. Inside a broken window of a nearby building on the second floor was a fluent and rapid heartbeat. Heavy breathing interceded silence as a body inside the warehouse structure came to life.

Cyrus was slumped over on top of some broken down packing boxes. His eyes opened and a sense of frustration cut across his face. But without fear or any doubt in his eyes Cyrus stood up. He may have been lost with no previous memory, but he somehow knew exactly where he was going. His instincts and intuitive nature guided him along every step. Cyrus showed no emotion and made no attempt to gather his thoughts while in the strange and unknown setting. Suddenly without reason, a look of force and corruption was scowled on his face, something outside the norm for his usually zen-like persona. He kicked open the blocked door of the warehouse and caused the door to fall outward on to the sidewalk. Cyrus continued outside and into the gloomy docile streets. He walked to a nearby street corner and looked for any familiar landmarks. But for some reason he couldn't remember where he was from, or where he was going. As he approached the corner he noticed a commotion in the distance. Cyrus glanced over to see what appeared to be two masked men robbing a pawn shop.

They were trying to get in through the front doors, but were having a difficult time with the door. Cyrus just watched.

"This is too much fucking work!" The shorter of the masked men shouted. "Let's do it my way!"

"You're way will get us caught for sure!" His partner yelled back. The stubby gunman reached into his black nap-sack.

"Shhhhhh! Nonsense. It's precise and effective. We'll be out before anyone gets here." The confident robber wound up and slung a brick through the glass window of the pawn shop. The window immediately shattered into millions of pieces onto the concrete below.

The shiny black locks of Malivick seemed to glisten in the moonlight as the shatter woke him from his slumber. He was propped against a pile of logs in an alleyway not far from the warehouse and pawn shop. Malivick stood up, but unlike his brother, he seemed dazed and took him a bit of time to shake off the cobwebs from being unconscious for seven days.

Malivick began walking in the direction of the disturbance while at the same time desperately trying to grasp his surroundings and why on earth was he was dressed in a blue robe. He reached the corner and noticed that two masked gunmen stood right next to him and were looting the run down pawn shop. His instincts kicked in and Malivick didn't think twice. He immediately stepped inside the front of Webber's Pawn Shop.

"Hey, what do you think you are doing?" Malivick asked. "Get out of there or I will call the police!" He startled the robbers, but they seemed confident that the intruder was not a concern. The stubby robber pulled up his mask to reveal what looked like another mask from his long bushy facial hair. He couldn't help but to laugh at Malivick's attire.

"Well don't you look cute in your gown? The beauty parlor is just up the road, but I think its closed." Both of the robbers broke into laughter. The taller of the two stepped closer to Malivick.

"I don't like your attitude... Boy!" The robber said, as he gazed into Malivick's clouded eyes. The robber slowly pulled out a pistol from his jacket pocket. But Malivick saw the gun and took a step back. The other robber lunged at Malivick and sliced with a long razor sharp blade.

Before Malivick could think of what to do next, he intuitively ducked a swing of the blade that came uncomfortably close. He swiftly responded with a direct kick to the thief's throat that put him on the ground.

The robber wielding the gun didn't even get a shot off from his pistol before Malivick leaped incredibly high into the night sky, out of sight. The stunned gunmen looked up in astonishment as the inhuman like figure landed on top of him, and snapped his arm in half. The gun fell to the ground and, Malivick stepped away from the thief as he yowled in pain.

"You son of a bitch!" The robber sobbed as he fell to the ground. His comrade was back to his feet and now had pulled out his own gun.

"Dodge this!" The enthralled robber fired two shots at Malivick, but just as he did, Malivick took a step forward. With just a raise of his palm Malivick suddenly slowed down two live rounds and just pushed them aside. Malivick was just as stunned as the robbers. The bullets whisked away once again at full speed.

Without further hesitation Malivick wrapped his leg around the confused gunmen and tripped him up. Out of anger Malivick dropped his fist forcefully into the back of the gunman's head. The robber's bearded face shattered on the concrete.

Malivick lost control. He could not understand what had become of him. A look of deep emotional pain came over him, as he caught a glimpse of a shadowed figure that stood in the distance.

Malivick no longer wanted to fight, and ducked out to a nearby alley way. He peered back around the corner to see the figure was approaching his location. The large brick building gave just enough cover to remain hidden. Malivick glanced into the store window, and viewed the reflection of his face. His eyes glowed red in the darkness.

What the hell? What am I?

Malivick stared at his sharp incisors and thought to himself. On the brink of breakdown, Malivick began to mumble to himself. "Selfish....What is happening?" Malivick wandered by an old half demolished church that gave an awkward chill. He brushed the thought off and stumbled onto the sidewalk. Malivick looked up at the crescent symbol that was haloed by the moon above the church. Malivick choked up and had a hard time catching his breath. He collapsed onto a nearby bench next to the dark empty street. The only street lamp that worked was that above the bench. It barely broke the darkness around Malivick.

Back at the Pawn Shop, the shadowed figure stood over the two injured robbers. At first the sight of the looming image frightened the pair, but soon their fear turned to desperation. The figure leaned down to one knee.

"Help me." The robber groaned as he cradled his broken arm.

The figure moved into the light and hovered over the robber.

"It's you... It's you!!" the robber that he was seeing the face of his attacker, but instead it was Cyrus.

"Your pain and suffering is minuscule in scale and comparison to that which I will unleash on your family." Cyrus told the terrified criminal. His eyes burned bright red as he picked up a large shard of glass from the sidewalk. He stood over the broken arm bandit and taunted him methodically before he held the glass high over his head. Cyrus thrust down onto the pavement and gorged the man through the chest.

"Judgment day is at hand for the race of fools." Cyrus laughed to himself as he raised to his feet. His clothing along with his demeanor had changed. His long black coat cloaked him fittingly as he stalked away in the night.

CHAPTER FIVE

"The Eternal Vow"

"Philosophy : A route of many roads leading from
nowhere to nothing."
- Ambrose Bierce

The full moon began to drop beyond the horizon of the nearly demolished church. Malivick sat calmly on the street side bench. His gaze was focused in front of him, into the dark of the night. Suddenly a mysterious figure cloaked in white appeared next to him.

Without turning to the figure, Malivick spoke -- somewhat disturbed.

"What's happened to me?" Malivick asked. "I can't remember anything," he had trouble finding words. "But... I feel that I've changed."

To Malivick the cloaked figures voice reverberated like that of a deity. The figure had a total void for a face other than red eyes that glowed much like his own. "Time, will answer that question best, Malivick." The figure told him.

"Malivick? I am Malivick? How did you know that?" He questioned further. His face became pale as his fears became reality.

The cloaked figure bellowed the answer to Malivick's journey. "You have been chosen as a protector." The figure said. "I have been sent to guide you along the path to salvation."

"I don't understand." Malivick fired back. "Am I a vampire?" He wasn't sure if he wanted the answer. There was a brief pause by the figure, but soon continued to dissuade Malivick further.

"A vampire, yes." The figure answered simply. "But do you even know what a vampire is?"

A grim snarl ripped across Malivick's face. However his eye contact continued straight forward with no movement. He seemed almost hypnotized. "Vampires are murderers!" Malivick yelled. "They kill for blood. It's an endless cycle." His expression calmed once again, clouded by confusion.

The cloaked figure again fed his propaganda to the vulnerable yet dangerous Malivick. "You are looking through your human eyes when you recognize a stereotype such as that Malivick." The figure said. "Vampires are a race unto themselves, and they want the same freedoms that humans have fought for. They haven't always hunted for blood. Where do you get your ideas about vampires?"

Malivick seemed confused. "I... I don't know. I just feel..." He was interrupted.

"Listen, you have to close these thoughts out and really listen to what I am telling you." Malivick felt these words were useless. However his mind was fragile and the cloaked figure seemingly had a mental hold over him. Malivick's eyes closed and he was taken away to a dream like world.

"History Lesson"

An enormous palace sat atop the dunes in what is the modern day Kingdom of Saudi. Inside and out the palace was immaculate and pristine by any standards. Aramaic symbols adorned the pathway to the palace walls. Gold trim covered everything inside from the floors to the ceiling as far as the eye could see. This palace was home to a ruler who used currency to gain and remain in power.

In the throne room of the royal palace one amenity was even more astonishing, a massive solid gold statue adorned the courageous warrior turned ruler Elias Julian the Third.

The flesh of this being sat slouched atop an exquisite personalized throne. At his feet were two female servants to adhere to his every demand. Malivick felt his life force hovering in the room, but the cloaked figure's voice bellowed forth. "Thousands of years ago even before the Greek empire, Elias Julian III became a powerful ruler who conquered millions and spread his greed across the entire western hemisphere." The figure faded in and out of reality. "His army was by far the largest in the world. They were fearless and unbeatable."

Malivick could imagine the strength of a vampire army. His body and spirit seemed to grasp his situation more clearly. The cloaked figure continued his passage.

"Soon Julian's army was threatening the rest of the world population if they did not accept him as their king and savior."

History played itself out in front of Malivick. "But soon his greed and lust for power angered a powerful wizard and protector of the Earth named Cisec." The images in front of Malivick began to change as a staggering white light entered the palace throne room.

The powerful wizard Cisec entered through main doors guarded with Elias Julian's highest ranking warriors. Cisec continued at a steady pace right up to Elias Julian. More of Julian's soldiers rushed in behind him.

"He confronted Julian to his face and demanded that he forfeit his power and return the lands to the people." The tone in the cloaked figure's voice changed.

Elias Julian jumped to his feet with an angry look of dishevelment and he demanded that his men take Cisec away.

"But Julian didn't want to hear a word Cisec had to say." The voice bellowed. "He threatened to have Cisec imprisoned. But Cisec knew the evil truth behind Julian's power and rule. He had studied a regenerated spawn of human DNA, that Elias Julian used in transfusions that created the vampire race." Malivick's new ally seemed to stump him with all of this knowledge.

Malivick was even more confused than before as he became aware of his sedated state. "He was searching for a way to become immortal. Those of his followers he infused with his plasma grew to incredible strengths, speed, and cunning." The figure said.

Malivick's eyes opened and the visions disappeared. They were again on the bench, in the dark.

The cloaked figure concluded his lesson even though Malivick seemed to be growing bored with the lack of real information.

"In essence Elias Julian was the father of darkness," the figure proceeded with the intensive history lesson. "He was God of the vampire race. But Cisec was going to make sure that Julian could never hurt another person. He bowed at Julian's feet and recited a prayer created to seal the evil rulers fate. The prayer was bound with the curse of eternal darkness."

Malivick couldn't take it anymore. "Stop it!" He shouted growing more frustrated, but still he remained seated with eyes deadlocked in front. "I don't even know if I can trust you. All of this is just... too much."

"Just listen." The cloaked figure again faded in and out of reality. "Cisec was prepared to die there with Julian to ensure his death. He did what he had to do to protect the planet. The curse he placed on Julian was return karma for Julian enslaving the human race." The cloaked figures voice paused checking that Malivick was following. "The curse would trap Elias Julian underground, but would keep him alive." he told Malivick. "The trick was that all of his hunger for greed and power would shift into something much worse. He would now lust for blood. Trapped in rubble, stuck alone, he consumed himself eventually committing suicide in the most heinous way you could imagine. Cisec knew that Julian would get what he deserved."

The cloaked figure seemed to loose his grip over Malivick. "I think I've heard enough." he said finally. Malivick broke his lifeless stare and looked to his side where the cloaked figure was seated, but the figure had vanished, even though his voice echoed even louder.

"What Cisec didn't know was that because all of Julian's followers were transfused with his plasma, when the curse infected him, it ran through his bloodline also affecting all of his followers." The disembodied voice continued. "And, that is why they must have blood. And, that is why you are here." The figure was gone, but his heavenly voice rang loudly.

Malivick was in a nervous panic, but was able to pull it together. "Thanks for your help, but I'm going to go now." He said. Malivick tried to stand, but a golden halo appeared around Malivick on the bench and lit up all around him. The halo acted as a force field that restrained Malivick in his seat.

"Where are you going to go?" The voice asked. "You don't have a home anymore Malivick. You have not stumbled through these streets and here to me by any coincidence. You are here for a reason."

"And what reason is that?" Malivick retorts without thinking it over.

For a moment there is no answer. "I think that you already know, until now you've just been afraid to acknowledge it."

Malivick does know.

"You are here to fight for the existence of the human race." The voice was exceedingly more aggressive than before.

Malivick relaxed his muscles and stopped fighting back momentarily in attempt to reason with the powerful acquaintance. "Hold it, why would I fight for the humans if I am a vampire?" The halo dissipated around Malivick.

"You haven't always been a vampire." The disembodied voice bellowed.

"Well what does it have to do with me?" Malivick asked. "And what's going to happen to the humans if I don't fight?" Malivick seemed more intrigued, or else just wanted to get it all over with.

"I know there is much you want answered, but right now time is short. The process is already in motion." Malivick looked around for the figure that spoke to him.

"I'm attempting to keep an open mind here, but you are making it extremely difficult to do so." Malivick said. "I have no memory before five minutes ago, and you are telling me that I am a vampire and I will hunt for blood, but I won't die in sunlight. Oh and I'm supposed to defend the human race. Do I just about have it right?

WHAT POWER DO I HAVE!?" Malivick's aggression was exhausted.

"Silence!" The disembodied voice sent an electric current through Malivick's body. "You have the equal power and maybe greater power to the one man that is going to try his best to destroy the human race."

Malivick interrupted. "Elias Julian?" The electric piercing went away.

"Not exactly. It's your brother, Cyrus." The voice echoed for what seemed an eternity.

"I have a brother?" Malivick asked. "I don't understand. Why would he..." He had a difficult time digesting all of the information at once.

"Elias Julian's followers believe that he did discover a way to become immortal before being killed," the voice continued. "They believe that by killing off the humans by a certain day that it will resurrect Elias Julian, and release the curse bringing immortality to him and his followers."

Malivick's demeanor evidently became more serious. He knew what he must do, but still questioned his abilities.

"What is this certain day they plan to do this?" Malivick asked, swallowing hard unnerved by what might come next.

"It is written in the scriptures that the massacre of the humans would start three days before and last up to the new year 2032 according to the Avinalen calender." The disembodied voice bellowed. "They believe that this day would come and this is what they must do to get there. Thousands of years later, they want their god back."

Malivick stopped struggling. He just wanted real answers. "How long until 2032?" Malivick's voice was weakened from the torture.

"A little less than five days." The voice replied. Malivick was shocked. He had been unconscious for a week, with no prior memories. And in five days he had to stop an army of vampires from destroying the planet.

"What? I..." The disembodied voice interrupted Malivick's confusion.

"I understand that there are many answers you are still searching for. But you are not ready!" Color finally began to return to Malivick's face as his energy was replenished. "Now, just a few miles from here, down this road is a safe house. It's a place where your kind lay their head for safe rest." The voice echoed away from Malivick as the street light above Malivick flickered out and left him lit by only the subtle moonlight.

Malivick shot to his feet still with many questions racing in his mind. "Hey what do you mean my kind? Aren't you a vampire too?" Malivick asked. He was all alone. The figure seemed to have dissipated into the wind as if never to exist.

Malivick sighed in discontent in the answers he had received. He started off all alone down the empty street.

CHAPTER SIX

"A New Underworld"

"The doom of a nation can be averted only by a storm
of flowing passion, but only those who are passionate
themselves can arouse passion in others."
- Adolf Hitler

C yrus approached the entrance of the church with a crescent symbol engraved in the door. A demonic organ piped from deep inside the desolate synagogue.

Cyrus looked up and down the building and took a final glimpse of the sacred symbol of vampire immortality. He pushed the door inward and entered the temple. He stalked slowly in the darkness.

Cyrus noticed an oil lamp that hung by the entrance. He searched around in the dark for a flame, but came up empty. He moved along the narrow hallway that led to the prayer chamber, and took the oil lamp along anyway.

Four large marble tables embellished the front of the prayer chamber. They took up much of the ground space in the main chambers. A single flame from the top of each marble platform streamed calmly giving off a concentrated luminance. Cyrus ignited the oil lamp with one of the flames. It lit up the entire room.

Two beastly figures hung above him in the rafters of the room. Cyrus turned around holding the lamp higher. The vampires leaped down directly in front of Cyrus.

The larger of the two was a beast in size. He stood nearly seven feet tall. His devilish features along with numerous piercings brought shivers to any sane persons spine. The mammoth vampire approached Cyrus, while the smaller of the two took a methodical approach. "Who do you think you are trespassing here?" The beast asked. "Do you know who runs this place?" His voice was forceful and demanded an answer. Seemingly of Hispanic dissent, the smaller bare chested beast showed off his tattoos on his chest and arms. Another large tattoo of bloody knuckles covered his entire back.

Underneath the ink it read,
'Bare Knuckle Boxing Champion'

Just in case he wasn't heard clearly, the largest vampire stood right in Cyrus' face. "Diox asked you a question." The beast said. He thought about it for a second. "Forget it. You made a big mistake coming in here."

Cyrus was not hesitant to speak up. "You know who I am and why I am here." He told them. "I am a man that creates my own destiny. What about you? Damian."

The large beast stepped back at the mention of his name. "What do you know?" Damian retorted.

Cyrus seemed to soothe the uneasy spirits of the vampires. "The spirit of Elias Julian has sent me to you." He said with a slight grin. "We are all here for the same reason." Cyrus' words purged the confusion from the vampires expression as two more shadowed figures jumped down behind him. Cyrus could sense the two and he turned his head slightly to speak to them. "We must resurrect our god!" Cyrus shouted as the two figures stepped into the light.

Leander, the smallest of the vampires had a visible scar running down his left cheek. His smaller stature allowed him to use his agility and quickness to elude enemies. His style for a vampire was quite odd. He enjoyed wearing torn clothes and crazy hair styles. The taller and eldest vampire, H. R. Gray was the leader of the group easily sensed by Cyrus' intuition of power over the others.

Cyrus turned to face all of the vampires. "You will all serve as my followers in bringing back our father!" Cyrus said to the group. Damian and Diox cut a sly glance at one another as H. R. Gray extended his hand to Cyrus.

"You have our allegiance until the end, Cyrus!" Gray exclaimed and smiled with satisfaction. "I see you are ready for the new year. I was just reaffirming what it is we are fighting for, studying the Avinale Cipacol and showing Damian how important these hours are." Gray paused as he thought about the war to come. "You know, Damian is truly a remarkable beast in strength and dexterity." He continued. "However, he's young and has a difficulty grasping the FUNCTION in all of THIS! We must guide him in the right direction." The two exchange a long stare.

Cyrus' powers were effectively manipulating the others minds. "Say no more Gray," Cyrus replied. "I want to speak with you about the light of Elias Julian. In his final days Elias secretly discovered the fate that was awaiting him. He was so established and intuitive he foresaw the curse that Cisec was mastering. Hours before he was captured Elias proclaimed to his followers that he would return after death. He said that his return would be marked by an amazing show of lights in the sky. In the scripture it says Elias would burn a hole in the sky five days prior and up to his resurrection."

Cyrus turned away from Damian and walked out of the room.

He stopped before walking back into the room. "Are you coming or not?" Cyrus led the vampires back through the main corridor and down a narrow hallway.

The contingent of vampires made their way up a stair-well onto the church's rooftop. Cyrus looked back into Damian's eyes and continued his previous exposition. "Elias said a constant white flame would burn over the location of his burial ground, over the five days leading up to the new year, the light would grow smaller and more luminescent over the location that our vampire god is located." Cyrus turned away from Damian and pointed to the sky to the east and there just as Cyrus had described the white flame like light burned a small circle in the sky. "Do you see?" He asked Damian. "The scripture reads the truths of our past, as well as our future. It holds the key to the world -- Our world! We are going to unlock it, Damian. Together. It's the way it was written." Cyrus' words seemed to offer answers to life's most complex mysteries.

Damian's face lit up with intrigue. The mood was extremely powerful for this dangerous bunch. Damian looked into Cyrus' profound glowing eyes. "Tell me one thing Cyrus," Damian paused. "In the Avinale Cipacol, it reads that when Elias returns to Earth, the prayer of eternal death will be lifted, and we will all become immortal. Is this true?"

Cyrus didn't break eye contact with the giant. "Yes." Cyrus replied with a smile "That is all Elias Julian ever wanted for his people. Power and eternity! Damian, we have five days until the new year." he continued. "No apocalyptic prediction could foresee the terror that we will produce in the next one hundred twenty hours. Humans and all who oppose us will be decimated in the most atrocious form and fashion. We will be sure that Elias Julian's resurrection and succession of world wide rule is the judgment day that no human could ever have imagined!" The crew was unquestionably stoked by Cyrus' words of encouragement.

The scar-faced vampire stepped in from the darkness with an opportunity for the new found alliance.

"Cyrus, there's a place down town, the Loch." Leander said anxiously. "It's where the low life vampire scum go to hide from the rest of society. The cancer of our race, the walking contradictions. They plan on trying to stop us anyway. I think we should show

44

them what they are up against!" Leander was ready to fight. And they were all ready to kill, but Gray shook his head, "Take it easy Leander." He tried to calm the eager vampire.

"What do you say Cyrus?" Damian was on board and wanted to know what Cyrus thought of the idea.

After a benevolent pause much like a calm before the storm Cyrus cracked an evil grin. "Let's raise a little hell, shall we?" He exclaimed with brutal aggression.

The group brimmed with confidence and climbed back inside the church and down the stairwell. The extremely thorough H. R. Gray led Cyrus into an artillery supply room. The room was stocked with masses of explosives, guns, blades, and other types of devices for demonic dismemberment. Cyrus cocked back a shotgun, and loaded up on ammunition as the vampires prepared for war.

CHAPTER SEVEN

"The Dream – My Nightmare"

"I have spread my dreams beneath your feet. Tread
softly because you tread on my dreams."
- W. B. Yeats

A deafening female scream pierced the silence of daybreak as Malivick's hand touched a large sliding steel door to the Loch. Malivick stood silent with panic before quickly pulling his hand back from the door. He listened intently for any other signs of life. Malivick looked around for another entrance.

No windows, no other doors. *Great.* Malivick picked up what used to be a chopping axe, but the blade had been broken down to its wooden handle. He slammed the handle against the rusted lock securing the facility. He slammed it down again and again. Finally, the lock broke into two pieces and fell to the ground. Malivick entered the eerie building and was met by the stench of death.

As he entered the Great Hall, his breathing became louder, deeper, and more frequent. The hall was very dark and difficult for him to see. Soon Malivick came to a set of double doors that he pulled open. Inside was the main sermon area, along with his worst fears. Masses of dead and mutilated bodies were piled up in the sermon pit. Everything had been destroyed and at least fifty brutally dismembered and slain vampires littered the area in a horrific scene of violence.

Malivick hesitated a moment trying to keep his composure. He promptly concealed his panic when he heard the same female cry for help somewhere inside. He pulled himself together and moved through the sea of bodies, stepping over and around death and up to the second floor loft area where a young female vampire was impaled through a spike mechanism atop the devilish device of torture. She was still alive even though she was pierced right through the chest and connected to the wall. The female vampire whimpered with her final breaths as Malivick noticed even more dead bodies on the upper floor. He desperately looked around for a way to free or at least comfort the dying woman. Suddenly the smell of smoke filled his lungs. Malivick looked up and realized the roof was on fire. He knew he didn't have much time.

"What happened here!?" Malivick wanted an answer from the dying vampire even though he wasn't sure what he could do about it anyway.

"I... Saw them come in." she tried to speak, but blood filled her mouth, and she coughed even more. The fire spread quickly from the roof to the rest of the building.

"Saw who come in? Who!" Malivick panicked even more as the carbon monoxide engulfed the building with no windows or exits.

The female vampire cleared her throat. "I saw him..." she was fading fast.

"Who did you see!?" Malivick shouted as he tried to shield her face from the deadly fumes.

"Elias Julian." the female vampire said. Her words burned Malivick more than fire ever could. He tried to free her from the spike, but realized movement would only further the damage.

"That's not possible!" Malivick shouted to the vampire, he obviously was looking for a different answer.

The female vampire struggled to get the words out. "I saw him!" she paused to clear her throat of the dark red almost black blood. "He told me to tell you that the end is near." the young vampire faded away in his arms. Malivick's eyes welled up with tears. He looked up just as a large portion of the burning roof collapsed next to him, but was able to dive away just in time to avoid being crushed. Malivick realized it was time to make a headlong exit. However when he reached the door and pushed outward it wouldn't budge. The door was blocked from the outside by fire charged roofing.

He pushed and smashed at the door, but before he could escape, another large portion of roof above Malivick collapsed. He dove to escape but the burning debris landed directly on top of him.

Moments later sirens rang out in the distance, as fire burned around and on top of Malivick.

****

Malivick and Cyrus stood as children on the front lawn of their family home. They tossed the football around with their father, Olympus. Malivick went out for a long pass and caught it. He hustled back over and all three stood together.

"You know boys, you're still young now, but I can see that the lord has something very special planned for the both of you." Olympus told them. "I am so proud that you are my sons, and no matter what happens, whatever you two talented individuals do with your lives, I'll be watching proudly."

Olympus' words echoed as the beautiful sunny day in the yard turned into a terrible storm. Malivick whipped around and now stood deep inside a densely forested area. He had his adult figure back, but now was running in fear of a figure that was chasing close behind. No matter how fast Malivick ran, the figure closed in right on him. They dodged trees and hurdled shrubbery until Malivick stumbled and fell.

The figure caught up and his face came into view. It was Cyrus. Right behind his brother was accomplices Damian, Gray, Diox, and Leander. A bright white light consumed Malivick's entire body.

Malivick opened his eyes and sat up in bed. He was hoping this was all a dream. He took an immediate defensive position just to be sure. The room was dark except for a fireplace that burned on the other side of the room. There were no windows in the room, but in the background the same cloaked figure from earlier sat calmly, his red eyes burned through Malivick in the darkness.

"Where... Am I?" Malivick spoke slowly to avoid detection.

"You're safe, don't worry." the cloaked figure said. "I hope I was able to help answer some of your questions." the resounding voice bellowed to Malivick.

"You mean the dream?" Malivick pulled his thoughts together and tried to figure out where he was.

"Try not to think of it in terms of a dream." the figure continued. "Try to think of it more like an extension of reality. Now you know what you are up against Malivick. Your brother Cyrus has been chosen by the Elias Julian to lead the rebellion to resurrect the deity back into power." the figure paused as if waiting for Malivick's next   question.

"How is that possible?" It didn't add up for Malivick, yet he tried to grasp the concept.

"Malivick, I know you better than you know yourself," the figure told him. "Same for Cyrus. Now, you were raised in the Christian faith. And in that faith do they not believe in the holy spirit and the resurrection of Jesus himself? Vick, I also know about your father, Olympus. I know that it was a difficult loss for you, and there will be a proper time to grieve. But right now it is time to fight." the figures exposition was interrupted by Malivick.

"Why doesn't God do something about it then?" Malivick asked. "Why would he let such an atrocity destroy his people?" He fired off more questions in an effort to piece together the puzzle of his life and future.

There was a long pause before the cloaked figure responded. "I can see you are the one to defend the good in this world, but you continue to clutter your mind with the intangibles that just do not belong." the cloaked figure lamented. "Think about this on a bigger scale, Vick. Anything can and probably will happen."

"You didn't answer my question." Malivick stood firm.

"The answer is more complicated than I can explain right now." the cloaked figure offered. "But I promise you will know the truths to your questions soon enough." As he paused, the voice of the impaled female vampire from the Loch rang out in Malivick's overwhelmed mind.

I saw him, it was Elias Julian.

"I went where you told me to go, and I found all the vampires dead, except one." Malivick said. "She told me that she had seen Elias Julian, and that he and his gang killed everyone." He delegated to his confidant all of his worst fears.

"It's quite possible that she saw your brother, only saw Elias Julian's spirit instilled in him." the figure shifted a bit. "It's hard to know what powers he possesses. He could have done that on purpose to frighten you."

Malivick jumped to his feet, eyes wide open. "So he knows I'm looking for him!?" he shouted. His alertness was raised by the thought of his brother hunting for him.

The cloaked figure also stood up face to face with Malivick. "I would imagine so." the figure told him hastily. He turned away from Malivick and with a raise of his ghastly white and glowing fist he extinguished the fire. "Now, I haven't quite figured out where they are yet but, Cyrus has assembled a clan of elite vampires who will act as his generals in the war." the cloaked vampire continued. "They have already begun to plot their course in which they plan to annihilate half of the worlds human population in the next three days." Malivick was stunned.

"Half!" Malivick shouted. He approached the cloaked figure with vigor.

"That's right." the figure continued. "This is why you must stop him before they have the opportunity to start killing. This is very serious. They are aimed at killing more than three billion humans. But don't be deceived, they will kill *every* human once Julian is resurrected." Malivick moved closer to the glowing vampire. Suddenly the figure vanished, and immediately reappeared away from Malivick at the opposite side of the room.

"The number is an equal ratio of fifty to one, for every vampire they are going to kill fifty humans. That is what it will take to break the curse, according to the vampire scriptures. They did their math and now they are poised to release the curse." the demanding figure bellowed. Malivick sat back down and cupped his head in his hands "Cyrus will have vampires killing in the streets on every continent." He continued to unleash the unwanted truth to Malivick's brooding mind.

Malivick raised his head in search of a more positive answer from the figure. "It's not my brother doing it!" Malivick yelled. "Where do you get your information?! You still haven't told me who you are!"

The cloaked figure attempted once more to convince Malivick of the path that had already been paved for him. "Malivick, to understand you really have to listen to what I am saying." He began. "Now, my visions this far have all come true." Malivick couldn't believe what he was hearing.

"Oh that's reassuring, your visions. VISIONS!" Malivick threw his fists in the air, wishing this were just a dream. "I'm going out there to fight an army of vampires based on your visions!" Much like the first time they met, Malivick wanted to leave. But again like the first time he could not find an exit. While searching the darkness for a door or any other way out, Malivick came upon a large black book with gold text that glowed in the darkness and read, 'Avinale Cipacol'. The cloaked figure floated over to Malivick who was on the other side of the room.

"How do you think I found you?" the figure probed his subject's emotions further. "It was no coincidence." Malivick flipped through the glowing scripture for a moment before turning around to face the figure. "There are more than one hundred million vampires on this planet. Most of which have been lurking in the shadows of the underground. Until now. Once Cyrus and his crew start hacking up bodies, word of his presence will spread and you can believe that when it does millions of other vampires will get in on the act." The ominous threat of total annihilation began to settle in as Malivick's face grew more pale than before. He shook his head and couldn't believe he was in this position.

"Since the vampire scriptures were discovered and studied, all vampires follow the word in that book and they want their father back. Only death -- is going to stop them." the figure slightly dissipated. "I'm afraid that when this massacre starts, there will be no stopping it. You are Cyrus' equal, the only one that can stop him!" the cloaked figures exposition rang familiarity back into Malivick's mind.

"How am I supposed to stop him?" Malivick became flustered as he fought to free his mind of the invading thoughts. "I don't know where he is, and I'm sure if he has all of these followers behind him like you say he does, then I have no chance to get to him." he was really aggravated at every answer that seemed to open up more questions.

"You must *kill* him." the vampire put it simply. "And I believe you will soon learn where to find him." Malivick didn't want to think of the obvious, for it was likely the most painful.

"What? Maybe I don't want to kill my brother. Maybe I decide not to fight." Malivick offered an alternative, but he was interrupted by the cloaked figure before he could finish.

"You're wasting time! I already know that you will fight." the vampire said. "The project has already been put into motion. You will fight. But you will not fight alone." the cloaked figure was transparent in the darkness and his glow permeated Malivick's entire body. He looked at the figure in one final accord.

"There is a warehouse, back up town near the church that burned down." the figure told him. "It's going to take a little work to make it, but there you will find what will be for the next four days your closest allies. They will assist you in creating and implementing an immediate plan of action to stop Cyrus and his forces of evil." the cloaked figure disappeared and Malivick panicked once again, "Now WAKE UP!"

CHAPTER EIGHT

"Awake"

"All men dream but not equally. Those who dream by night in
the dusty recesses of their minds wake in the day to find
that it was vanity; But the dreamers of the day are
dangerous men, for they may act their dream with open eyes
to make it possible."

– T. E. Lawrence

Malivick's eyes opened and awoke from a deep slumber. He batted his eyelids heavily to focus the blur all around him. He realizes he must have been sleeping for quite some time. The plain white room was spinning around him as sounds from a news report played on the television hanging in the corner of the room.

He began to wonder how much of this has been a dream. The female news reporter presented the breaking news, "Tonight in Downtown Remington Park, a subsidiary building belonging to the Faith of the Surviving, burned to the ground," she reported. That answered one question. "A spokesman for the local police say right now it appears to be an isolated incident, stopping only before calling it an accident. He also said that they have turned the investigation over to the Federal Authorities."

Malivick shook off the cob webs and pulled himself together. His concentration shifted back to the television reporter.

"The Remington Park area has been undergoing renovations for over ten years, economic struggles have hampered the project, leading fewer people to occupy the coastline town." she continued. "One eye witness was able to confirm that one live subject was pulled from the fire. The witness account says that she saw some sort of armored vehicle that looked like a mobile quarantine unit that was used to transport the survivor, who authorities say is now in federal custody." the news reporter continued the discussion on this subject as Malivick grasped reality. He *was* the subject. Upon realization of his situation, Malivick sensed two armed guards just outside his room. His breathing and heart rate increased as he pulled the I.V. from his arm, and the heart monitor patches. The machine began beeping, but the guards were unable to hear. Malivick hesitated for a moment, then quickly hopped from his bed.

Just on the corner of the bed was a tray with needles and other medical tools. As he stood, Malivick bumped the bed and the pan fell to the ground. The guards outside the room were alerted and approached immediately.

The guard directly outside the room turned to face Malivick with his M-16 fully automatic rifle. He was instantly cut off when Malivick smashed the heart monitor right across the soldier's face. The soldier went down and without missing a beat Malivick reached back and lunged his hospital bed into the doorway as the second uniformed soldier rushed toward the commotion. The soldier was caught off guard as the bed on wheels left the ground only to smash him in the face. A few wild rounds from his rifle went off as he dropped to the ground.

The first soldier came back for more, but Malivick's instincts were firing on all cylinders as he sidestepped the soldiers' attack. Malivick grabbed his opponents gun and wrapped the soldier's arm up, breaking it viciously at the elbow. The soldier whaled in pain inadvertently firing multiple rounds as he collapsed to the ground. The erratic gunfire luckily shot the second guard between the eyes, killing him instantly. The soldier continued to scream from the pain of his fractured arm.

"Take two of these and call me in the morning." Malivick silenced the injured soldier by stabbing a syringe into the each side of the soldiers neck pumping air into his veins. For a moment, Malivick was motionless and silent.

Malivick took off down the hallway and blazed by another testing facility where two doctors came out and yelled for him to stop.

He didn't stop. He ran around a corner and saw three more guards coming toward him. He ducked behind the wall to stay hidden. They approached his immediate location, but Malivick was hidden well enough to go undetected. Seconds later he caught the armed guards off their step. Malivick lunged from behind the wall and landed a solid high kick to the leader's throat. The soldier fell in to the other two. Malivick grabbed another guard that was loaded with full assault gear including an M-16 assault rifle. Malivick disarmed him and used his body as a shield, as the third gunmen fired three shots.

The guard was killed instantly, and his lifeless body slumped to the floor. The guard fired more shots without hesitation, but Malivick ducked backwards onto his hands as the shots whisked over and killed the stunned vampire. Malivick grabbed the guards gun and with one swift motion fired two shots at his final opposer. Malivick looked all around at the damage he had inflicted. He dropped the gun and continued his escape from the compound.

Malivick rushed out the doors of the main entrance and through the gates outside of the covert government-protected triage center. The Sun burned as he got outside. It made him nervous as it seemed brighter than ever.

He ran off down the road to the nearest alleyway, and only paused a moment to look around to ensure he wasn't being followed.

Back inside the compound dozens of soldiers were being notified of a breach, and within seconds they converged on the vampire's trail.

CHAPTER NINE

"Cyrus' Specialists"

"Evil brings men together."
        - Aristotle

Just beneath Malivick's feet in the underground was the evil that plotted to derail his mission.

A station in an abandoned subway system served as converging grounds for Cyrus and his followers. In addition to his closest servants, were two dozen other vampire supporters.

Cyrus stood atop a large platform above the legion of vampires. Standing to his right were Roth Rhodes and the lovely Venezuelan beauty, Eva Cordez. Eva seemed innocent but was as brutal killer as she was beautiful. She enjoyed nothing more than to watch the slow painful death of her fallen enemy. Her long black hair was pulled up and kept neatly under a black military cap.

Roth was a careless and aggressive vampire that was down for whatever and would go the length for Cyrus when needed. The two stood in the front of the pack and listened closely to Cyrus' specific commands.

"Servants of Elias Julian. Quickness will be the key as we progress through the first day of the war. We must make an impact in the first hours as we move through the cities." Cyrus' voice resonated with the followers. "We must kill everyone in our path. Upon successful completion of the ultimate goal numbers, I believe thousands more vampire will follow us to our truth and reconciliation. And you all will be the leaders. My disciples." Cyrus paused when his vampire soldiers gave a confident cheer.

"This will be one constant onslaught until our goal is met. Once you are joined by reinforcements, destroy any military opposition that remains intact and no matter what happens do not stop!" Cyrus' orders were clear.

"And if military reinforcements do get there in time, what saves us?" Roth asked just to what everyone was thinking, although he spoke only to hear the sound of his own voice.

Cyrus didn't have time for games. "Your God will save you! Are you listening?!" Cyrus turned to Roth and spoke slower. He seemed even more emotional. "Kill. Them. All!"

His vision was evident as the vampires were ready to kill on a seconds notice.

"With pleasure!" Roth shouted. The group seemed to be on the same page.

Diox stepped forward from the middle of the pack. "Cyrus, how will we know when our goal is met?" he asked.

Cyrus leaned in to address his people. "Our suffering will be avenged when blood rains from the sky." Cyrus points to the heavens. "That is when you will know that our savior has returned to this earth. That is when we may all claim a stake in our new world. Now you will all return to the streets to spread the word. Elias Julian will be resurrected on the new year! In just four short days we will be FREE! Remember, the element of surprise will be our greatest weapon." Cyrus shot a glance at Damian.

"Well, second greatest." He corrected himself. "Now all of you, go and spread the word!" with that the flock ascended to the surface as Cyrus' central unit of hunters gathered.

"Now gentleman, and lady. Cyrus and I have decided who will go where." H. R. Gray said as they gathered closer. "We have specific files for you to help understand your location and what will be expected of you." Gray stepped forward and handed the paperwork to Cyrus.

"Leander, you will fly in to Bombay, India." Cyrus kept eye contact with him. "Your path will take you northeast across the most densely populated areas of humans. Roth, you will stay with me here in America to eliminate the biggest pest." He drifted off into a daydream of the disgust for his nemesis, while Gray continued Cyrus' thought.

"Damian, you and I will touch down in Lisbon, Portugal where we have a large underground movement of vampires that will move east through Spain and France." Gray laid out the game plan for each vampire general.

"We believe that is where we will face the most resistance. Eva my dear lady, you have the distinction of turning South America to extinction. You will fly into São Paulo, Brazil in the coastal area of the South Atlantic Ocean. We have a group waiting for you in the nearby city of Santos." H. R. Gray winked and gave Eva a devilish grin before continuing. "My good friend Exodus is already on the Gold coast in Australia gathering the local vampires there and is awaiting our signal." Gray stated.

Cyrus nodded in approval of Gray's command. "Diox you are going to Morocco, more specifically Casablanca." Cyrus told him giving Gray a moment to go over the paperwork. "You will fly into Mohammad V International Airport and link up with forces in the north. Now, we will all depart tonight. Are there any questions?" Cyrus offered an open forum for the closest of his faithful.

Leander stepped forward, "What if your brother tries to get involved?" he asked. The mention of Malivick almost sent Cyrus into a tirade.

"He will!" Cyrus stated promptly. "I am positive that he will be looking for me. But don't worry, Roth and I will take care of him."

Roth wanted to calm the situation. "Cyrus, I just want to say it's a pleasure to be working for you." he's interrupted by Cyrus.

"You are doing this for Elias Julian, remember?" Cyrus asked, pointing his finger in Roth's face. "When you go out there to kill and maim, you make sure they know why they are dying. You make sure the last thing that goes through their head is how the vampire race is taking control of Earth forever, so that when they are met in the afterlife they can tell their God the stories of how his kind was destroyed." Cyrus continued.

"The light of Elias Julian grows smaller, but burns stronger by the minute. And by the minute we too grow stronger." Cyrus' poisonous words spread to the vulnerable vampires. "As we stand together for the last time before we meet our God face to face, I tell you now we will have a grand stake in the new world. The curse of eternal darkness will be lifted and we will all finally be free of the tyranny created by the humans." The troops were confident and more than ready to get into battle.

CHAPTER TEN

"Last Hope – The Battle Begins"

"You must be the change you wish
to see in the world."
- Mahatma Ghandi

Malivick stood outside the Slyte Warehouse in a nearby rundown part of the mega city. This block in particular was known by those familiar to the area as the Slums of Barabos. It was mid day and Malivick was cloaked in a long dark coat, and black sunglasses. He couldn't seem to figure out why there was never anyone around. He searched around the exterior of the building before approaching the enclosed alley that led to the rear entrance of the desolate back street warehouse.

Malivick pulled the heavy steel doors outward. He hesitated a moment thinking about his safety, but soon proceeded inside and not to be scared a bit, he closed the door behind him. The glaring sun shined through the blacked out windows just enough for Malivick to see where he was walking. He shuffled his feet down the corridor trying to find his way, when his mind was suddenly jolted with images. Images that seemed to be from the future. The images more specifically were of faces, and they hit him all at once. Along with the images came information that flooded into his mind. Oddly enough it comforted him. The faces were those of apparent friendly vampires who had been sent to assist Malivick on his mission. He moved closer to the center of the warehouse and soon reached the a single door at the end of the hall. Malivick touched the handle and felt the same shock as before at the old church. This time the feeling was different and he felt strangely comfortable and calm, so he proceeded through the open the door.

Malivick peered inside and saw four vampires in a meditative state. They were hovering above a marble platform that stood three feet above ground level.

As he stepped in he could see these were the faces that flashed through his mind. Adrian Suvarro, Cassandra Reinold, Nike Wells, and Colin Grimm were the names implanted in Malivick's mind. He seemed in shock as he slowly moved closer to the vampires.

Adrian nearly thirty years of age was in his prime physical peak, had no noticeable weakness, and was Malivick's closest peer intelligence wise. His fiancé Cassandra, with her quick thinking, blazing speed, and sharp shooting skills was an asset to the group as well. Adrian and Cassandra hooked up two years ago when they began training for the mission.

Nike Wells came from a human military family from France, while Colin was born in New Zealand and was extremely agile, with unbelievable physical strength that rivaled the rest in the group.

A voice echoed inside Malivick's mind. "Welcome Malivick. You seem on edge. Don't worry, you are safe here." Cassandra's soothing voice comforted Malivick and he relaxed his guard. "We are grateful for your joining us."

"Who has sent you all here?" Malivick's thoughts transmitted brainwaves frequencies to the others in the room.

"Right now, we must skip formal introductions in order to save what precious time that remains. I know the answers are important to you." Adrian transmitted amongst the others.

"It is important to me. It makes no sense. Why did Cisec turn me into a vampire and have us fighting to save the humans?" Malivick asked hesitantly.

He was immediately answered from the self-assured Cassandra. "You have been chosen by someone with greater power than Cisec. You have become a vampire to counter the transition that Cyrus has undergone. You are the exact counterweight of your brother in the balance of good and evil." Cassandra responded.

"We have been sent to help you stop the rebellion." Adrian said in thought. "Meditate with us Malivick. Help us locate the evil that is soon to plague our planet. Together we can stop Cyrus before his evil consumes us all."

67

Malivick felt at ease with the creatures, more so than he could remember anytime before. So he sat with the others and, although he was unsure how he was able to think what the others were thinking, Malivick focused his energy on the task at hand.

Random visions began to race through Malivick's mind. Suddenly, the groups' thoughts projected upon the walls of the room. One of the images was of Cyrus and a few other recognizable faces vampires in front of a wall tagged with a familiar image.

"What is he doing there?" Nike asked.

"It looks like Cyrus is still rallying vampires, spreading the word to as many as he can." Adrian stated the obvious.

"That's not good news." Colin weighed in on the issue. But Nike noticed something in the details of the background.

"Yeah, but I know the artwork on that wall." Nike replied. "It's at a club just outside D.C.." Nike was dead sure of what he saw.

Malivick was pleasantly surprised. "How soon can we be there?" he was ready to go.

"Well that depends." Cassandra came out of the meditative state and spoke aloud. "Do you want to drive or do you want to fly?"

Adrian led Malivick up the lift to the rooftop. The warehouse was outfitted with a heliport. A UH-60A Black Hawk military helicopter mounted with two M60D 7.62mm Machine guns sat atop the warehouse roof. There were more light weapons inside the chopper. Malivick armed himself and the others quickly followed. He made sure to grab a few extra grenades. "These should come in handy," he assured himself.

Adrian climbed into the pilot seat, as Malivick and Nike loaded up in the back. Colin and Cassandra stayed behind.

"Colin's going to stay here to work out the logistics in case things get out of hand." Cassandra shouted as the blades really got going. "I'll meet you guys there, I'll bring the Hummer." Cassandra and Colin headed back inside as the helicopter lifted off.

Outside Club Cameo in the dim commercial block, just off the highway, the sun began to set, and brought the new year one day closer.

Inside, Cyrus, Damian, and H. R. Gray sat around a circular glass table in the V.I.P. Room of Club Cameo. This room was quiet as the club below rumbled the foundation. Leander stood guard by the doorway as the four went over final paperwork of the war plans. Presentations of kill statistics by hour appeared on four large plasma televisions above the shimmering table.

"Do not unleash your units on the population until I give the signal." Cyrus told them. "Keep your radios open once you reach your destinations. I want updates every six hours from all of you." Cyrus persisted in getting his orders across.

"Cyrus, you know. I know, you know, that we have our ends covered. Spare us the mundane, and let's get started." Damian was anxious. He couldn't wait to start killing the humans.

Cyrus slammed his hand down on the table and turned to look Damian in the face.

"That's the attitude I'm looking for out there." Cyrus spouted to Damian who flashed a cocky grin at Gray. "Not in here."

"Sorry Cyrus." Damian backed down. Cyrus turned back to the television and viewed a world map that showed initial death rates, and from increasing infection day by day.

"What I am telling you here will secure us a victory," Cyrus turned to the others. "We have to reach our limit before the dawn of the new year or Elias will continue to be trapped inside his tomb for eternity."

"Now we have enough artillery to defend against the humans, and once word spreads in the underground all of the vampires will roam the streets killing and infecting them turning them into ravenous vampires, which in turn will bolster and increase our army against the human population." Cyrus continued to show facts and figures based on scripture as Damian mimicked falling asleep. Suddenly there was an obscure but noticeable rumble just outside foundation of the club. Cyrus didn't want to risk it.

"Leander, see what that was." Cyrus demanded. Leander was already off to see about the commotion.

Back outside the club, an explosion ripped through an extended part of the club and lit up the evening sky. Adrian navigated the helicopter onto the roof of Club Cameo, but a few dozen more vampire rushed outside and took aim at the chopper with mostly small arms fire. Adrian was forced to maneuver to a safer landing zone after taking heavy fire in the helicopter.

Nike laid down heavy suppression fire with the mounted M60D Machine gun, while Malivick wasted no time and bailed out of the helicopter. Nike quickly followed action as the gunfight began and quickly escalated to an all out brawl.

"I'm guessing this is the place." Malivick continued to dish out ass whippings to the first wave of attackers using the M-16's and close combat martial arts. The bodies hit the ground almost instantaneously.

Adrian navigated the chopper to a safe landing zone, hopped out, and joined the two.

Leander emerged from a balcony connected to the club and saw the destruction. He immediately bolted back inside to inform the others.

An eager vampire appeared on the rooftop with a rocket propelled grenade launcher on his shoulder, which only intensified the gun battle. He lined up his shot and immediately fired an RPG that whizzed by Nike and hit the helicopter dead on. The catastrophic explosion just meters from Malivick and the others sent a shock wave of burning debris that forced them to the ground.

Adrian got to his feet first and scrambled over to the others. "You okay?" he asked the two.

"Yeah. Nike?" Malivick brushed off the rubble and moved in on another flood of enemy vampires. Nike appeared from under some debris and shot off a few rounds and took down an approaching enemy vampire.

"I'm fine." Nike responded. "Let's get these mutha fuckas," the three quickly regained composure, and finished up the last of the attackers. "This way," he told Adrian. The three hustled to the back of the building. "Right up there on the second floor is the room where I saw them, they have to be in there." Nike pointed out. He reloaded and checked his gun as they made their way inside Club Cameo.

Malivick was bewildered at the sight of Nike readying his weapon. "No Wells, I want to talk him out of this." Malivick pleaded with Wells. "He will listen to me," he almost didn't even believe his own logic.

Adrian and Nike traded a look of confusion.

"No way. Malivick, we can't afford to risk this." Adrian tried to reason with him. "We have to kill him, this has to end tonight!"

"If we don't take him out, he is sure to try to take us out." Nike stated. "Like it or not Vick, I am bringing my gun." He loaded the clip and stood ready.

Malivick lowered his head. "Fine. But keep it put away," he knew it was the right decision. "I want to at least try to convince him what he is doing is wrong. If it doesn't work out. Blast him. Now let's go."

Leander entered the room out of breath. "Cyrus!" he shouted to alert the others of the invasion. "Malivick is here and he's killing our fighters." For the first time Cyrus was startled.

"Is he alone?" Cyrus asked.

"No. He's with two others." Leander replied with haste.

Malivick entered the room and interrupted.

"That's right. I am here, brother." Malivick came with good intentions. "I'm here to save you from your own lies. This will end tonight. But not the way you had hoped." Malivick moved into the center of the room followed by his comrades.

Cyrus looked confident now that he was in control. "You made a mistake coming here!" he shouted. "And how dare you liken yourself to me?"

"Just surrender calmly, you don't want to do this." Malivick offered a way out. He simply didn't want to have to kill his own brother.

Cyrus just laughed off his comments. "Of course I do," he replied. "No one here wants to listen to anything you have to say. And on the contrary, it is going to end tonight, for you and your friends." Cyrus paused. "Gentlemen. Kill them now."

Precisely at that moment Malivick, Adrian, and Nike dove to evade attack. They discharged their firearms to fend off the attackers, but Damian and Gray wielded large guns themselves.

Malivick fired off three shots blindly from a crouched position behind the liquor bar. Damian fired as many rounds into the bar hoping to hit his foe. Full liquor bottles shattered and the liquid and glass rained down on Malivick's head. He's had enough.

Damian watched in surprise as Malivick leaped onto the bar and flipped forward using his hands to spring board himself over into Damian. He kicked the gun from Damian's hand, dropped his own gun, and moved in on the monstrous beast. Malivick landed a few kicks to the abdomen, but that did not phase the remarkable brute. Damian countered a quick punch and then, with one of his own, Damian sent Malivick and himself through the glass table. The table smashed into millions of pieces, but the gunfire didn't even slow up.

Cyrus was either using mind games to taunt his opponents, or he seriously had a death wish as he sat calmly in his seat. He didn't flinch or move a muscle as three separate fights intertwined and circled the room.

Nike Wells was tucked down behind the large plasma display and used it for cover while H. R. Gray continued suppression fire. They all knew they had to kill Cyrus, but if one of them stopped firing at his generals, they would all be dead in an instant. Suddenly, the situation went from bad to worse when two more of Cyrus' closest followers entered the room to help out. The trio held their own, but soon even more vampires from the club entered and things got out of control. Cyrus, Gray, and Leander ducked out of the room and left their soldiers to fight for them.

Malivick disarmed and disposed of two vampires before he stunned Damian with a high kick to the throat.

"Malivick! Go after them! We'll meet up with you downstairs in a minute!" Adrian used his quick thinking to turn the situation around. "Don't let them get away!"

Malivick didn't hesitate and sprinted full speed in pursuit of Cyrus and his followers. He reached the balcony just in time to watch a Chevrolet Camaro drive off carrying the H. R. Gray, Leander, and Cyrus.

Soon after a black Hummer slid into the parking lot next to the busted and burning helicopter. Cassandra emerged from the Hummer. "What did you do to my chopper?" Malivick didn't know if she was serious or not. He could muster no good excuse. "Ah. I -- didn't do it." was his offering.

"We have to catch up with them, come on." Adrian said. The groups focus was concentrated on the black Camaro far off in the distance.

Adrian approached Cassandra as she was about to get back in the drivers seat. "You made it here fast." he gave Cassandra a kiss while the others loaded up in the Hummer.

"Couldn't wait to see you." Cassandra said smiling. She jumped back in the drivers seat and sped off after their enemy.

H. R. Gray was behind the wheel of the Camaro while Cyrus rode shotgun. Leander stared out the back seat window as Diox sped past them on a black motorcycle and pulled far out ahead of the speeding Camaro.

"Where is Damian?" Leander asked.

Cyrus wasn't worried. "He'll catch up." He could see in the rear view mirror that the Hummer was slowly gaining on them.

"They're following us." Leander said while reloading his gun.

"Of course they are." Cyrus exclaimed. He pulled out his communicator. "Roth. Are you at the airstrip?"

After a brief pause, Roth's voice came back over the airwaves and confirmed he was in position. "Good. Where's the plane?" There was a slightly longer hesitation before the reply.

"It's right on time, coming along soon now." Roth responded.

Cyrus was not thrilled. "The plane is not there yet?" he asked while keeping an eye on the approaching Hummer."

"Uh. No. No, it's not." The transmission ended.

"I put you in charge of providing transportation to be at the airstrip." Cyrus said as he became more intense and aggressive. He threw the communicator onto the dash.

Roth came back over the air waves. "But you weren't supposed to be here for another hour." Roth replied, but Cyrus didn't want excuses.

"Change of plans." Cyrus shouted into the communicator. "We'll be there in ten minutes, now find out where my plane is!"

The Hummer was gaining ground on the speeding Camaro, when suddenly a motorcycle appeared a few hundred feet behind the Hummer.

Cassandra was behind the wheel and Nike looked back at the motorcycle that pulled up quickly on the group. The rider fired a few rounds from his sub machine gun that hit the rear quarter panel of the Hummer.

"Shit! Someone's shooting at us!" Nike shouted as he put his head down and grabbed his gun.

"Shoot back!" Cassandra yelled. She swerved to avoid the shots. Adrian turned around in his seat and took aim. "Hold on!" she shouted as she cut the wheel sharply to the right. Cassandra slammed on the brakes in an attempt to collide with the motorcycle. The attempt failed and she floored the accelerator to evade the gun wielding cyclist now identified as Damian, Cyrus' thug from earlier.

Again she attempted to run Damian down, but her repeated attempts failed, all the while Nike and Adrian fired numerous rounds at him. Malivick took aim at the Camaro and fired off a few more shots.

From seemingly nowhere two more masked motorcyclists appeared, this time strapped with large Kevlar bullet proof vests and fully armored helmets. One of the cyclists fired shots at the drivers door of the Hummer. Cassandra at the same time swerved to the left and ran the biker over.

"I'm hit!" Cassandra shouted as she leaned over the steering wheel. Adrian looked down as blood poured from her chest.

"Get her in the back Adrian! Hurry!" Malivick yelled as he grabbed the steering wheel and hit the accelerator with his left foot. Bullets were still penetrating the doors of the Hummer, Malivick was sure he was about to die. Cassandra made it to the back seat as Malivick slid into the drivers seat and maneuvered to avoid the heavy automatic gunfire.

"Are you alright!?" Adrian was worried, but did his best to care for his injured fiancé.

Now that Malivick had taken over the driving duties Wells had to worry about taking fire from multiple directions himself. Nike continued spraying bullets at the two motorcyclists, but the Hummer was still taking shells from the Camaro as well.

Cassandra got an idea of the severity of her wounds.

"I'll be fine," she pulled herself together. "It barely hit me."

"I need some help Adrian!" Malivick said as he shot from the drivers side window. He watched as the other motorcyclist idled up to the side of the Hummer. Malivick shot at him, and hit the rider in the helmet two times. But the bullets just ricocheted off causing little damage. He swerved left but the biker maneuvered around the back of the Hummer to the passenger side where he pulled up directly next to them.

Simultaneously all four passengers aboard the Hummer looked over at the rider and realized he was strapped with explosives. He opened his vest and tugged on a cord hanging from the device.

SHIT!

The device detonated causing a massive explosion that ripped a hole through the Hummer and sent the vehicle flipping out of control and off road. It rolled five times before it finally came to a stop. It was lodged upside down between a dead Loblolly Pine tree and a recyclable dumpster.

The Camaro didn't even slow down, but Damian pulled the motorcycle to a stop near the wreckage. He noticed something move out of the corner of his eye and immediately fired off shots in proximate vicinity. Damian heard a clinking sound that could only be one thing. He looked away only for a second, glanced back to the Hummer and saw Malivick duck behind the wreckage. Damian looked down to see a grenade at his feet.

"Oh fuck!" Damian tried to duck behind the motorcycle, the only nearby cover, but Malivick fired in that direction and forced Damian to the ground as the grenade exploded.

Malivick searched through the wreckage in search for the others. Cassandra had a light gunshot wound, and the others were also slightly injured by the collision. But they were all alive.

Nike got to his feet. "That was some ride." he muttered.

Malivick helped Cassandra up, but then remembered Damian was probably still alive. He looked over to where Damian went down, but he wasn't there.

"Keep your eyes open, he's gone." Malivick said looking around by the tree and wreckage as Nike dialed away on his cell phone.

"Colin. Come get us, we uh... Ran into a problem." Nike said. "Good, alright," he hung up the phone and carefully navigated to Malivick. He touched his head where the most pain was and felt blood. "Colin tracked our location, he's already on his way."

Adrian approached the two with Cassandra at his side. "Did you see which way he went?" Adrian asked but Malivick was clearly shaken and simply shrugged.

"I didn't even see him get up." Malivick replied. He picked up the motorcycle, and checked the bikes durability.

Adrian knew what Malivick was thinking and handed him a nearby helmet. "Malivick, you have to catch Cyrus," he told Malivick. "We will be fine here. Go after him."

Malivick nodded knowing what he must do. He hopped on an early twenty-first century Ninja 650R crotch rocket, and burned out in hot pursuit of the Camaro.

Roth stood nervously on the empty airstrip. He held a Halliburton briefcase. A few more laid next to him. Eva was beside him looking into the sky. With his free hand Roth pulled out a slim cell phone and put it to his ear. "What the fuck do you mean you don't know where the jet is?!" Roth screamed. "We paid you to pick us up in a jet RIGHT NOW, now where the FUCK is my jet!?" He was severely irritated and slammed his cell phone shut.

"Roth, Cyrus is going to be here in two minutes and he has no where to go." Eva stated. "He is going to kill us!" she reassured the already informed Roth of his fate if his jet didn't show up in time.

"I know this!" Roth yelled and paced back and forth holding his head.

Meanwhile, Eva looked away into the sky and caught a light in the distance. "Roth... Look!" Eva yelled. "There's our ride." She grabbed one of the iron briefcases.

"Right, alright then. We're back in business!" Roth was relieved. The plane circled the area twice, then dropped the landing gear. It slowly descended on the single unlit runway.

Inside the Camaro, Leander and Cyrus noticed the motorcycle gaining in the distance. They unloaded their guns at the approaching enemy.

"Shit! It's Malivick. He must have taken Damian down." Cyrus said. He feared that he had lost one of his best.

"What now?" Leander turned in his seat to ask.

Cyrus wasn't sure what to do next. "Kill him or we're not going to make it."

Gunfire ricocheted off the Camaro right next to Gray's head. "We're almost there. Someone just take him out!" Cyrus shouted.

Gray pulled out a semi automatic pistol. "I'll take care of him." Gray checked the clip; and he was locked and loaded. He aimed out of the drivers side window and shot four times and the bullets ricocheted off the fuel tank of the motorcycle slowing Malivick down.

Malivick was stunned by sparks from the gunfire. He shot back at the car, but his automatic rifle stopped firing. "Shit!" Malivick threw the gun down and sparks shot from the road as the gun skidded to a stop along the pavement. Malivick reached by his side and felt for the weapon he noticed earlier. He removed a sawed off shotgun and with one hand cocked the weapon and took aim.

Back inside the Camaro, Gray took aim at Malivick once again. The car sailed over a curb and crashed onto the grounds of the old airstrip. Only a few hundred yards from the plane, the Camaro plowed through the gated area that protected the unused airstrip.

Malivick was gaining.

"SHOOT HIM!" Cyrus looked at Gray bewildered as he hit the breaks and cut the wheel. The Camaro was sent into a spin, Malivick was coming full speed as the car spun face to face with the damaged motorcycle. Gray closed one eye, aimed, and pulled the trigger twice at the exact moment Malivick unloaded a shotgun round that demolished the windshield. The car continued to spin back around to complete a full revolution.

The explosion from the shotgun shell ripped apart the interior and left smoke filling the car.

The front tire of the motorcycle shredded away and at over ninety miles per hour, Malivick sailed head first over the handle bars.

"Oh good stuff! Nice shot Gray!" Cyrus was amazed. He knew his brother was still alive, but at least they were safe for the time being. Thats when Cyrus noticed blood splattered on the side of Gray's face. "Is that…" Cyrus looked closer to inspect. "Blood?" Cyrus turned around to see Leander shot in the head.

"Fuck!" Gray shouted with despair. "Damian now Leander!"

Malivick laid bloodied face down on the concrete barely able to watch as the Camaro drove aboard the taxing Gulf Stream Jet. Unable to move, he just watched as Damian passed on another motorcycle. He must have thought Malivick was dead as he continued ahead and wheeled his motorcycle onto the plane. The jet finally left the ground, along with all hope that remained inside of Malivick.

Inside the cockpit of the large Gulf Stream Five, Cyrus entered with a smile on his face. Further back in the payload area, Damian dropped the bike down and saw Leander's body slumped in the Camaro. "What happened to Leander!?" He shouted. "Cyrus!" Damian's friendship with Leander had grown in recent weeks.

"Get us to the checkpoint." Cyrus relayed the instructions to the pilot as he went back to the payload. "Malivick killed him," he told Damian blatantly. "We'll have to go on without him. All of your flights will be waiting when we arrive at the check point." Cyrus turned to Roth. "The plans have changed," he said. "You're going to Bombay in Leander's place. Call Nephtali and tell him to meet me in the city." Cyrus straightened out the plan after considerable damage from his brothers efforts. He took a seat at the front of the plane and gazed out the window still slightly in a state of bewilderment.

CHAPTER ELEVEN

"Searching For A Plan B"

"In these matters the only certainty is that nothing
is certain."
- Pliny the Elder

The crew returned to the Slyte Warehouse with the mindset of imminent defeat and were feeling the effects of battle. Malivick along with the others used the time to recoup and plan a new strategy.

The boarded up windows shelled out the moonlight of the main room where the group sat uncomfortably and waited for the bad news that the war had started.

Three bullets dropped one by one into a glass jar. The clinking echoed in the tight enclosure. Cassandra gasped deeply for air as Adrian cleaned the wounds.

Malivick sat next to Colin by the computers, while Nike meditated. Colin was typing away at the keyboard, searching for any news on the invasion, but so far, nothing. Malivick placed his hand on Colin's shoulder and reassured him of their advantage over the enemy. "We have to be resolute, Colin," he said. "We can not believe for even a second that we have failed. As soon as you think it. Then it will be done." Malivick left Colin to the computer and approached Adrian as he finished bandaging up Cassandra. She seemed to be fine.

"How's that feel?" Adrian asked. "Better?" He cared for Cassandra and while their affection was evident, they were certain to never over do it.

"Yes. Thank you." Cassandra said. "Much better." she smiled and hopped down from the marble slab.

"Malivick, have you found anything?" Adrian turned to him. Malivick wanted to have an answer, but he didn't.

"No. Not yet." Malivick said as if certain to go on with a long speech about how they would find an answer. But instead Cassandra chimed in.

"What makes you so sure that this isn't meant to be the end of everything?" Cassandra uncharacteristically denounced their cause.

Adrian gently touched her hand. "Cassandra. Why," he didn't understand.

"Cyrus is the only one we need to focus on." Malivick said. "He is controlling the others minds somehow." He felt strongly of his beliefs even without having seen any logical proof.

"You're wrong." Cassandra interrupted. "They are following Julian. Besides what can we do now? You let Cyrus get away."

Malivick sensed something was amiss. "I didn't let him get away. I *tried* to stop him." He attempted to explain himself, but again Cassandra fiercely interrupted.

"Quiet!" Cassandra demanded. "What exactly will killing him accomplish? We are vampires. We will just be slaves to the humans." The others considered if she could be right.

"And do you think they would do the same for us?" Cassandra asked. "No! They would make sure every last one of us were dead." Her face lit up with anger as Malivick tried to keep the situation calm.

"There is more to this war than resurrecting Elias Julian and killing the humans." Malivick told her. "There is a bigger picture here. I just haven't been able to piece it all together yet. But I feel soon we will know the will of god." He was as sure of his words as anything he had ever believed.

Cassandra jumped to her feet. "Maybe this is his will." She said looking directly into Malivick's eyes.

Nike came out of his meditative state momentarily and approached the commotion. "Vick, I'm getting an incredible amount of hostile energy," he alerted Malivick of his meditative findings.

"I'm not surprised." Malivick mused. He leaned over to Nike so that Cassandra could not hear.

Ryan C. Stith

Nike followed Malivick's lead and relayed further information. "The activity was here," he said. "Inside the room." Malivick's suspicion was correct.

Adrian was also somewhat worried about Cassandra's current state. "What are you saying?" he asked her. "You don't believe that." He tried to hold her hand, but she pulled away and stood atop the marble slab and placed herself six feet above the others.

"I believe what I am told to believe." Cassandra said as she stared blankly at Malivick. "Just as everyone else before me." She paused before going into a total fit. She almost seemed possessed. "The complete and total annihilation of all humans will soon begin and you all know that will allow Elias Julian to take back what is his." Cassandra continued as Malivick's concern became evident. He approached Cassandra who by now was shaking violently. She seemed to be sustaining a subconscious physical pain and could not wake up.

Malivick knew that his brother was behind this somehow. Adrian looked at the others for some help, but Malivick continued to battle the overtaken Cassandra.

"If Julian is resurrected, it will destroy him, along with every last one of his disciples." Malivick spouted as he hopped up onto the adjacent marble slab.

"That's not true. You lie!" Cassandra yelled. Her shaking stopped. She leaped across the room to avoid Malivick's touch.

"Cisec bound the prayer of eternal death in case the location of his tomb was ever discovered." Malivick leveled with her as he again tried to get within arms reach of Cassandra.

87

"You're wrong!" Cassandra screamed. "Nowhere in the scriptures does it read of such a demise." She became more active with her movements. Still in trance, she gazed blankly as she spoke.

"You don't understand." Malivick elevated his tone. "I can see it clear as day on the tablets. The original Avinale Cipacol," he tried to be honest with her. Cassandra began to hyperventilate, but still remained unaware of her physical state.

"Malivick! Stop." Adrian demanded of him, but Cassandra interrupted.

"You lie!" Cassandra said as she fell to one knee. With utmost anger in one last deep breath she heeded a final warning. "I will destroy you Malivick!" she screamed in his face. "Have no doubt about that. Elias has plans for you if you try to interfere. The death march starts tonight, tell your friends."

Adrian was in shock and looked to Malivick who closed his eyes, looked at Cassandra, and saw something that shocked him; he could see a negative image of Cyrus speaking in Cassandra's place. Her hyperventilation increased and soon Cassandra collapsed onto the ground with a thud.

Adrian was the first to jump up on the slab to aid her.

"Wake her up." Malivick snapped at Adrian. He gently shook Cassandra to wake her from mental paralysis. At first his attempts failed, but soon was able to revive her.

Cassandra wept in Adrian's arms, as Malivick hopped down, and without mentioning a word about his vision, he headed for the exit. He stopped just before leaving the room. "I'll be back." Malivick said. Adrian turned as the door shut behind Malivick. He was gone.

CHAPTER TWELVE

"Realization Of Truth At Last"

"In time we hate that which we often fear."
                    - William Shakespeare

Malivick crept silently through the dim wet streets stalking cautiously in the darkness. Rain beaded off of his long black coat as he approached the crescent symbol that hung above the Unholy Temple.

Two vampires armed with sub machine guns guarded the entrance to the temple. Malivick concealed himself in the shadows of night. Behind him on the other side of the road an unknown figure followed close behind. On pure instincts Malivick suddenly leaped inconceivably high over the main gates and disappeared into the night sky. One vampire that was guarding the door got a surprise when Malivick landed on top of him and snapped his neck immediately.

The other vampire fired a few rounds at Malivick but he ducked away, grabbed the gun from the broke neck vampire, and fired multiple shots that eliminated the remaining vampire foe. Malivick ran up the stairs and kicked in the door.

He made his way into the darkness of the temple without hesitation. His mind wandered with angst as he journeyed deeper into the halls of torture. The walls were lit with multi-layered fire and burned concentrated all the way up the sides of Malivick.

Further inside the Unholy Temple, Cyrus stood before an enormous statue of Elias Julian.

It seemed he was talking to himself or perhaps facing inner conflict with the spirit of Elias Julian. "Why have you chosen me?" Cyrus thought out loud. "I don't want them all to die," he pulled at his own emotions. "Don't interrupt the balance! But, Why me?" Cyrus almost broke down. "I will not stop until blood from every human has been spilled!" He began to shout louder. The large door that led to the prayer chamber screeched open.

Malivick appeared in the doorway just outside. The vast circular room had a wide array of weaponry hanging along the walls.

Cyrus jumped to his feet with his back to Malivick. "So you finally came." Cyrus said.

Malivick stepped into the room. "You were waiting for me?" Malivick asked as he walked closer to Cyrus. He observed his situation and surroundings.

Cyrus took a step away from his brother. "Of course," he paused. "I couldn't wait to kill you!" Cyrus leaped over to the wall nearest to him where a long sword swung from the ceiling. Cyrus smoothly ripped the sword from the scabbard and wielded it, ready for battle.

Malivick followed his brother's lead and grabbed a broad sword from the wall. "Well then I guess this would be your best opportunity yet," he offered up. "Don't think I'll make it easy." He swung the blade around with striking accuracy taunting his brother. Malivick was astonished by the high level of skill displayed by Cyrus as well.

"Oh, but I will make it easy." Cyrus always had to have the last word as he grinned and stepped away.

Two masked vampires swung down from the upper balcony of the room. They were mounted on individual hanging rope swings that launched them into battle. They were wielding extra long samurai swords and slashed at Malivick as they swooped by, but he jumped just in time to avoid being chopped to pieces. The blades seemed enormous. They must have been four and a half feet long. Malivick wandered what he did to get himself into this mess.

"Just what I wanted to see." Malivick grumbled to himself. The two vampires ran along the walls of the room and had Malivick surrounded. He again dodged their attack. He swung his sword, slashed, and dismounted one of the vampires from the rope.

The pair dueled in a dynamic display of classic swordsmanship, parrying one another's attacks as the other vampire swung back around to him. Malivick fended off his attackers long enough to kill the fallen vampire in front of him.

Suddenly from another set of doors two more of Cyrus' loyal following entered. They, too were on the prowl for Malivick's blood. The seven foot tall vampire beast swung his over sized double edged axe, which resembled an ancient Arkalochori. The second of the two donned a pair of short swords. Malivick grabbed and latched on to the vampire swinging by. He reached for the rope but almost lost his grip so he pulled the vampire down and beat him to death with his bare fists, even before the other two could reach him. The difficult battle ensued as his opponent's Axe slashed right through his sword. Malivick dove away from yet another swipe of the deadly weapon. He fought to his feet and taunted his enemies as the vampire spun the short swords in his hands like toys. Malivick threw two daggers from the wall, but barely missed the swordsman's face. The monster handling the axe landed a devastating kick to Malivick's face that knocked him to the ground. The vampire stood over Malivick who was somewhat stunned but could still see a glaring opportunity as the sword wielding vampire closed in. The giant axe swung down right on top of him, but Malivick somehow managed to grab his opponents sword with his bare hands and pulled the swordsman down in his place. The axe severed the vampire at the throat, but the brutal giant didn't even hesitate after killing one of his own. Malivick immediately dove to avoid the next swing of the axe which was almost as lethal as the last. He ducked out of the way, then landed a kick that stunned the brute. He maneuvered around the much larger vampire and decapitated him with an accurate but desperate swing of his sword.

Cyrus and Malivick made eye contact and were dead locked and ready to rock. They wasted no time with words, only a long connection through eye contact before Cyrus lunged at Malivick and started the stunning battle of swordsmanship.

Both combatants displayed intense emotion and passion for their causes. After a brief yet intense standoff with the swords that circled the room, Cyrus landed a sudden high kick to disarm Malivick and smirked as his brothers sword slid away on the ground.

Malivick flipped up onto his hands and with his legs grabbed Cyrus' sword right out of his hand. They rolled around on the ground jabbing fists into one another. Malivick kicked his brother off of him and Cyrus collided with the wall. He looked up and grabbed a spiked mace that hung above him.

Malivick jumped up and attempted to retrieve his sword. He ducked a swing of the mace that barely missed his throat. Both brothers took a swing, Cyrus' mace wrapped up Malivick's sword and flung it from his hands. He was defenseless and his brother was not going to waste another second to end his life. He needed to think of something quick, Malivick rolled out of the way of a swing of the mace that nearly dismembered him, and rolled backward leading his brother to the edge of the room. The next swing of the mace got lodged into the stone structure and gave Malivick an opportunity to grab his weapon.

Malivick gained the upper hand and took a swing at his brother but Cyrus ducked out of the way. Malivick continued to thrust his sword at him and finally Cyrus stepped away. He ran out of space as he bumped against the wall. Malivick took a final swing, but Cyrus again pulled a slick one and whipped a sword out of the wall to parry his brothers advance. Cyrus lifted his leg and landed a tremendous kick on Malivick's stomach that knocked him to the ground. Malivick countered and swept Cyrus' legs. As Cyrus fell Malivick kicked the sword away from his hand. Malivick held the sword to his brothers throat.

Cyrus just licked his lip tasting the blood then spit it out. He stared into Malivick's eyes. "So, what are you waiting for?" Cyrus asked. "Kill me. Brother." His words triggered an intense reaction.

Malivick had an ill-timed flashback from the airport just before the brothers flew home.

Malivick and his brother laughed together in tune with one another's thoughts. Back when they were truly free spirits. One memory played repeatedly in his thoughts of him and his brother together playing their first game in high school.

Suddenly he was brutally brought back to reality. Malivick was in shock as he looked down to see he had been stabbed in the chest with a short dagger.

Cyrus kicked his brother off of him and got to his feet. "It's too bad it has to end like this," he whispered to his brother who was gasping for air. "You could have helped me eradicate this planet of the waste that you once were." Cyrus tried to persuade his wounded opponent. Malivick still had fight left but attempted to reason with his brother.

"And you used to be," Malivick said as he gasped for another breath. "Do what you must, but know this, when you resurrect Elias Julian, you will be committing suicide. It will kill all of us!"

Malivick's words fell on deaf ears. Cyrus let out a sinister laugh and stood over his brother for what he hoped would be the last time. Cyrus held the long sword right over Malivick's chest. "See," he hesitated. "I try to have a nice last moment with you and you have to go and ruin it by saying something asinine like that." Cyrus commenced the murder of his brother, but was interrupted when Colin crashed through the second story balcony window.

"Malivick!" Colin yelled down to his fallen ally. He wasted no time and fired three silver arrows, But Cyrus' incredible instincts were apparent as he sprang amazingly high to avoid Colin's attack.

Just as Colin reached the lower level to assist Malivick, Cyrus grabbed the rope swing and lunged himself to the top balcony, and to his escape. Colin grabbed the rope and followed back to the second floor. Even more glass shattered from upstairs. Malivick pulled himself to his feet, and held his wound as Colin returned to his side.

"He got away," Colin said. "What were you thinking coming here alone?" He was concerned about the integrity of the mission, but Malivick already understood his fault in the matter.

"I needed to finish Cyrus myself." Malivick offered.

"Yeah. Well if it wasn't for me, he would have finished you." Colin responded as he pulled out his ringing cell phone. "Yeah. What?" he asked. "Yeah I found him, I'm with him now. He's hurt." Colin shook his head. "What? Here, Adrian is on the phone." He put the phone on speaker.

"I'm here go ahead." Malivick spoke into the phone still bleeding from the deep wound.

"How are you feeling?" Adrian came back over the radio.

"I'm fine," Malivick knew that he wasn't fine. "What's wrong?"

"Cassandra tranced out again." Adrian told him. "She went quiet for a while and when she came to she said that she had seen the end of the war through Cyrus' eyes and that she knows the cities that his generals are heading to." The transmission ended and there was a deep silence.

Malivick thought of how to word his next question. "Do you trust what she says?" He waited on Adrian's response and hoped for something positive. Anything positive.

"I do Vick." Adrian replied. "And I feel that we have very little time to act." Malivick paused again to think about the importance of the decision.

He knew what to do. "Everything is happening exactly as it is supposed to." Malivick nodded.

"What?" Adrian's confusion was evident.

"Nothing," Malivick responded. "It's something someone told me once. Adrian, make the preparations. Colin and I will meet you at the place at the time."

Colin hung up and helped Malivick walk to the exit. On the way out he spotted a dead bolt that secured a room that seemed to lead outside. Colin took out his pistol and shot the lock off.

The room was totally dark. Colin flipped a switch that turned on an overhead light. "Looks like they left us a present." he said coyly.

Parked in the makeshift garage was the Camaro from earlier.

"It beats walking," Malivick touted. "Can you wire it?" Malivick hobbled over to the passenger side, while Colin climbed in the drivers seat.

"No need. They left the keys." Colin responded.

Something didn't make sense. "Why did Cyrus leave on foot if he had a car?" Malivick asked as he looked around for a way to open the mechanized bay door.

Colin fired the car up. "Does it matter now?" He stuck his head out the drivers window. Malivick knew the question was erroneous so he just hopped in the passenger seat. Colin peeled out and smashed through the flimsy bay door as they sped out onto the dark empty streets.

CHAPTER THIRTEEN

"The Race To Save A Race"

```
"While you are not able to serve men. How can you
serve spirits? While you do not know life. How can you
                know about death?"
                 - Confucius
```

Five brand new Gulf Stream G 550 jets sit parked in a row just outside a monstrously large archaic hangar. Nike unloaded weapons from a storage truck into one of the Gulf Stream jets as the Camaro sped in and power slid next to the planes. Adrian emerged from inside another one of the planes.

"Malivick, we have to go, now!" Adrian shouted. "We've already loaded the planes." Nike studied Malivick's wounds closer upon approach.

"What happened to you?" Nike asked him. Malivick pulled away. He tried to downplay his injury.

"Nothing." He said as he put his coat back on attempting to avert attention from his obvious weakness. But Nike prodded further.

"Are you going to be alright?" Nike tried to level with him.

Malivick just wisped back. "Of course I," he was interrupted by Adrian.

"Malivick, I want you to meet Archer Serafin and Batista." Adrian said as the two approached.

Archer was a tall slender man with sandy hair and noticeably had a lot of freckles. Archer may not have been much of a force of intimidation by appearance, but his recluse mentality and years of heavy weapon experience served justice to the group.

Batista was much bigger. His Greek black hair was slicked back and he had a look with little emotion that impaled his rigid eyes.

"Batista was the one who supplied the planes for us." Adrian continued. "Archer here, helped him steal them. They are human with the intent on staying alive. I believe we can trust them just as much as you can trust us."

Malivick's eyes wandered and was only half listening. But in a hurry he agreed to get on with it. "Fine," He said to them all. "I hope you know what you're doing Adrian." Malivick turned away from him, but Adrian grabbed his shoulder.

"Yeah Vick," Adrian added. "I want Batista to stay with you here so you have some help with Cyrus. He knows where Cyrus' men are starting from." Malivick didn't want to hear that Adrian had changed the plans.

"We need someone to go to Australia." Malivick said. "You said it yourself. Send him there to meet with the Atooq's." Malivick questioned his own words as the mention of the Atooq's sparked a fire in Adrian.

"How do you know about the Atooq's?" Adrian questioned Malivick further.

He tried to remember. "I - don't know."

Adrian came closer to Malivick so their conversation remained private. "Listen, the Atooq's can handle their lands," he said. "Cassandra said Cyrus isn't sending anyone there."

Malivick thought about it for a moment. "Cassandra said?" Worried he was making the wrong choices Malivick wanted to question Adrian's ability to make sound decisions about Cassandra. "You don't think I can take Cyrus on my own, is that it?" he asked.

Adrian swallowed the lump in his throat. "No, of course not," he reassured Malivick. "I just want to be sure. Just like you said. Cyrus is our main target."

"If you have something to say." Malivick told Adrian.

"There's no time right now."

"I appreciate your concern, really." Malivick turned back so that everyone could hear. "Batista is going Brisbane to meet up with the Atooq's" Malivick had his mind made up.

"Well then." Adrian said with a sigh. "I know what I'm doing. I hope you do as well Malivick." Adrian stood down.

Malivick tried to hold his tongue. "We don't have time for this. You just said it your self," he replied. "Is everything ready to go?"

Adrian gave Malivick a long stare. "We're ready to roll Vick." Adrian turned away.

Nike pulled Malivick's coat open once again revealed his bloody injury. "Are you sure you are good?" He asked again.

"I am fine!" Malivick shouted as he pushed him away.

Cassandra appeared from her jet for the first time. She transfered the last crate of ammunition then walked over to Malivick.

"How are you feeling?" Malivick sly started up a conversation.

"I'm sorry Malivick." Cassandra said. "I couldn't help it. He was forcing me to say those things. I didn't mean it." She seemed truly remorseful.

"I know," Malivick replied. "It was just a sign that Cyrus' powers are growing. That is why we have to act now." He helped her lift the other crates in the jet, but just the small amount of pressure on his wound sent him back into pain.

Adrian gathered the group. "Listen up everyone, the largest offensive will begin in Europe," he said to others. "Cassandra and I will be heading there. More specifically, The City of Seven Hills. Colin, Rio de Janeiro, Brazil is where Cyrus's top generals are planning a starting post in the city center." Adrian stared into Colin's eyes. "Link up with the human rebels in the area. They will welcome your assistance." Colin smiled in anticipation that he would soon be a hero. "Nike, your job will be to stop the rebellion in India, while Archer will do the same in Morocco." Adrian paused before continuing. "Batista that leaves you with Australia, I have faith that together we can all make the effort needed to stop the war before it starts. Colin downloaded all of the detailed information to your PDA's." He directed his speech to Malivick. "Remember, our efforts will only succeed if you are able to defeat Cyrus before the new year."

Malivick nodded and then proceeded with further instructions. "Get to your destinations as fast as possible and locate the offensive, that's where Cyrus' force will be found," he explained. "Eradicate the leaders of this group located in the thickest pack of vampires." Malivick's strategy hoped to catch Cyrus' crew at its weakest link. "Its not going to be easy. I won't lie. We are looking apocalypse in the face and now we must defeat inevitability. It is up to us to ensure our planet isn't destroyed by these tyrants." The words came from deep inside of Malivick, from a place he hasn't seen in recent memory. "The time is now!"

The final preparations had been made for the most ardent war the planet had ever hosted. Colin stood up and gathered his SAT COM and other belongings. "Well I guess this is it." Colin added. "The end of the line." He waited for the others to do something.

"I will take care of Cyrus. I'm leaving for the city now," Malivick said to the others. "Keep me updated, and don't stop for anything. Only when I send the message that Cyrus' is dead can we breathe easier." He jumped in the Camaro as the other six boarded the planes and readied themselves for flight.

"Good luck everyone." Nike gave one final farewell as Malivick peeled off in the Camaro.

CHAPTER FOURTEEN

"Checking Up On Destruction"

Lisbon, Portugal

J ust over the skyline in the city center of Lisbon, at the crack of dawn, the light of Elias Julian could be seen. It was now smaller and brighter than ever. The area was all quiet for now as beams of sunlight began to arc over the horizon.

A large contingent of vampires huddled around a downtown district where the humans would soon be on their way to work. Julian's followers were gathered to hear words of encouragement from Damian who along side Gray, approached the group.

Gray pulled the communicator to his ear. The voice was that of Exodus, one of the groups allies in the war on humans.

"Gray, do you copy?" The voice had a commanding tone over the radio waves.

"Go ahead Ex, I trust this a positive update." H. R. Gray looked around in approval from the larger than expected turnout.

"Everything is going according to plan," Exodus explained. "My assembly is ahead of schedule and we are moving forward into the city." His reply was short and to the point.

Gray was ecstatic with the report. "Already?" he asked. "That's sensational, I knew it was a wise decision to keep you in the loop. It doesn't matter what Cyrus says, you are important to this war, keep up the good work. Damian and I are just about to unleash our crew on these poor unsuspecting bastards. It's going to be so fun to watch. Keep in contact Ex. Gray Out." Gray turned his focus to Damian who gestured for the crowd of vampires to quiet down. They quickly obliged.

"Listen to my words followers of Julian." Damian said opening the address. "Your god will rise again on this new year. In just three short days we will be free of our restraints and enslave the humans." His powerful speech had an effect with the vampire cult. "Until that time we must flood the streets with the blood from every living human."

Gray was impressed with Damian's superior control. "Once we start we must move quickly. We cannot allow the humans military to take action and make a stand." Damian continued. "If you follow me, and listen to me, the pieces will fall into place as they are supposed to. With your cooperation we can bring our father back and release the curse that has bound us for too long," he signaled to Gray that he was ready to go. "After we have Elias Julian back in this realm he will have no use for the rest of these humans and will destroy them surely. Now go, and spread the word!" Damian stepped down and followed Gray away from the legion of followers.

Dozens of the vampires fired up chain saws which seemed to be the popular instrument for dismemberment among these vampire. The group began moving into the city and as they marched in eerie unison they began lighting fire to any significant structures that they passed. It was only a few moments before screams began ringing out in the distance.

THE NEXT PROJECT

Australian East Coast

Batista navigated the jet soundly through the sky, thousands of feet above the beautiful Eastern Australian coast-line. As the land mass came in to view Batista began searching for a clear landing zone somewhere among the destruction. Many of the larger buildings were already on fire and humans were fleeing from hiding.

Thick black smoke billowed up in to the atmosphere. The terrified humans were viciously slain by the vampires that marched in unison through the streets in a hellish demonstration.

Batista's reaction was a mix of fear and determination. He descended upon the target area and flew low, dangerously close to the chaos. The vampires on the ground looked up at the plane and knew the war was just beginning.

CHAPTER FIFTEEN

"Exodus Glory"

In the early evening on the streets of Brisbane, Australia, an American sports car sped by and slid out of control down a vacant street littered with dead mutilated bodies.

Just around the corner from the car was a pack of at least three dozen vampire. They wielded various weapons such as swords, machetes, pistols, explosives, rocket launchers, and others weapons. They were causing considerable death and destruction and left only dead mutilated bodies in their wake. The sports car came around the corner, screeched over the curb, and headed full speed at the line of vampires.

THE NEXT PROJECT

One vampire tossed a Molotov Cocktail at the oncoming car. The explosive bounced off the hood and ignited the roof of the flashy American car. It quickly spread to the fuel tank and there was an immense explosion that caused the car to wreck into the front of a nearby building.

Frightened citizens fled from the burning wreckage in an attempt to escape, but the vampires were relentless and sliced them to pieces with their vast array of blades. Their methods were atrocious and their terror was spreading faster than the humans could respond. The invasion had already become the largest organized uprising ever in America, or the world for that matter. Sirens could be heard approaching in the distance, but there was no success for the humans thus far.

Moments later a swarm of patrol cars sped onto the scene. Their training manual didn't mention how to counter a vampire attack. But instinct and will to live had overtaken the measures to protect and serve. The police moved in to action to try and quickly set up a road block in order to squelch the local rebellion.

The gun wielding vampires didn't hesitate a moment and began to unload everything they had at the police.

Exodus, the lead vampire in Australia saw the police draw their weapons and return fire. "Wait! Stop!" Exodus yelled. "Corino, get over here."

The police hit the vampires with round after round with no effect. Corino, a vampire equipped with a shoulder fired Israeli B300 rocket launcher ran over to Exodus and took a knee.

Exodus leaned over so that he could hear over the gunfire. "Take them out," he told Corino. "I want to watch them burn." Exodus just smiled even as lead and silver whizzed by his cranium. Corino aimed at the five story building that sat adjacent their position. The police were right next to it, so Corino aimed near the first few police cars.

He pulled the trigger and the rocket impacted between the first and second floors of the building at just the right angle. The devastating explosion caused the building to collapse over onto the human authorities. The fiery rubble engulfed the cars and trapped police inside, burning many of them to death.

Corino reloaded with the help of another vampire and fired a second rocket. It scored a direct hit on the furthest police car and caused three other vehicles close by to ignite. There was a series of explosions that engulfed the remaining infantry police and burned them alive.

"Beautiful!" Exodus shouted. "Now let's take the rest out, we have to keep moving!" He and a few others moved in on the police and decimated the remaining few. The monsters were able to eliminate an entire police squad in mere seconds! "Don't stop! Keep moving!" Exodus shouted. "We must continue into the heart of the city and then southward to our salvation and the extinction of these pathetic excuses for existence!" Exodus ensured the chaos continued, while above them the sky filled with thick black smoke. The vampires moved along the streets as the bodies piled up. Few humans remained alive in this virulent area.

More police arrived on the scene, but their efforts were instantly extinguished as three of the front line vampires, led by Exodus shot up the police cars. The heavy gunfire killed all of the remaining police.

Two more convoys of weapon toting vampires appeared from around the corner. One of the military style Hummers rolled by and Exodus jumped on board and loaded up on ammunition. The vampires had gained a hold in this city and remained in control for an eight mile radius and were continuing to move outward.

CHAPTER SIXTEEN

"In The Media"

"Law is mind without reason."
- Aristotle

Attacks began in the Eastern Hemisphere initially, though reports were scarce about the mass extermination. In Brisbane, Australia, where the first attacks were the most severe, a local news station was about to air the first footage from inside the attacks that would alarm the world wide general population as to just what they were up against.

Australian News Anchor Peter Nubins sat under the spotlights on the set and waited to go on the air. His producer stood out of view, and prepped him on the breaking news alert. The scholarly anchor adjusted his microphone above his black silk tie.

THE NEXT PROJECT

"Do we have a feed from the scene?" Peter asked. The level test sounded good. Peter gave the thumbs up.

His producer hung up the phone. "Not yet," he told Peter. "Make sure you tell them to stay inside." The producer handed a sheet of paper to the camera operator. He passed it along to Peter Nubins.

The camera operator took his place back behind the camera. "We're on in thirty seconds." He said while he adjusted the camera's focus. Peter's focus remained on what was going on outside.

"Who are they?" Peter continued questioning. His journalistic instincts prodded further investigation.

His producer didn't know much though. "All that we are being told right now is that this is some sort of rebel uprising." The producer said. He gave the signal to go live.

"We're on in five… four… three… two…" The camera operator led Peter in.

The veteran anchor gave it a moment and then began his report to the local community. "Good evening Brisbane, tonight our community is under attack," he began. "And while a vicious group of rebel fighters try and dictate our existence, the Australian military has already deployed a full regimen to the inflicted area." He paused waiting for the prompter to change. "Any motives, political, religious, or otherwise are currently unknown. Also still unknown is the number of rebel fighters in the attacks." Peter paused again, but this time to brief the citizens on a personal level. "Residents are strongly being urged to remain inside keeping doors as well as windows, locked. Our reporters are en route to the area, and we will have a full report live on the scene as soon as it becomes available." Peter hoped that he wasn't lying.

Ryan C. Stith

CNN Headline News Studios -- Atlanta, Georgia

The news of the worldwide attacks had just been discovered by the American News Press. Inside the news studio a live broadcast was already in progress.

CNN news anchor Martin Wills delivered the address to the broad audience in the United States and worldwide. "Some of the headlines seem less threatening than others. For example, Janook, a small town just outside of Bombay, India has a headline of their front page that reads, 'Masked Swordsmen Besiege Government Offices'."

Martin held up the paper and showed headlines in the native language. He put the paper down and looked at a second briefly before he held that one to the camera. "Yet in Germany, one of the more popular news agency reports are about to roll of the press in just an hour, 'Thousands Perish in Brutal Mass Murders - Numbers Still Growing'." Martin lowered the papers. "We don't know exactly what any of this means, and there is no official word that these attacks are linked, but the safe bet would be that they are coordinated together and that we could be seeing more of these terrorists, in other places around the world," the news anchor became more serious with his demeanor. "Right now we have no word of any other mass murders, however we have yet to be able to get anyone into the affected areas to see first hand what is going on."

THE NEXT PROJECT

Live feed from a German independent journalist rolls. He's directly in the center of the murders that are currently taking place in Lisbon, Portugal. The journalist, Nate Webber pointed to the large group of vampires for his camera operator to film. The horror of human murders and torture were broadcast unedited around the globe.

The group of vampires had already moved through the area and all that could be seen were dead and decapitated bodies and fires burning all multi level buildings to the ground. The two willingly in danger climbed on top of their news van and set up the camera. They faced the vampires who were approximately a hundred yards away. Nate was in shock as he suddenly felt unsure about being in his position. "I can't believe what I am seeing." Nate said. "These vicious animals. I would dare say human, are just maiming these poor people with no regard for life. They are showing no sacrifice... No mercy for the living."

Further down the road away from Nate and his assistant, being broadcast on live television was the two that led the hunt, Damian and H. R. Gray.

One of the vampires closest to the reporters turned enough to see the human spectators. He relayed the information to Damian whose face told Nate that it was time to go and was reassured when Damian yelled for the flock to attack.

The camera operator frightened to death stated no more than the obvious. "I don't think this was a good idea Nate." He said as the pair hopped down from the van simultaneously.

"Now is not the time!" Nate shouted as they scrambled to make their getaway, but within seconds a half dozen blood crazed vampires had reached the truck. The ferocious vampires rolled the van and decimated the two reporters while exhausting little effort. The two journalist howled in horrific pain that was displayed for the world to see.

Suddenly, the feed was lost.

Back in Brisbane, Australia, Peter Nubins' report continued on after the intensely graphic video footage. The live feed was a surprise even for the weathered and experienced Nubins.

"We apologize sincerely to our viewers that just witnessed a horrible, despicable act of rage and hatred against a national broadcast journalist out of Germany, once again that was in Portugal." Peter said seemingly shaken. "Remember, remain indoors at all cost. Those responsible for these acts are armed and extremely dangerous and should be evaded at all cost," he continued. "According to reports from citizens calling in the rebels are killing everyone and destroying everything in their path. We still have no motive, and no idea who these murderers are. Yet they have managed to kill over seven hundred ten thousand people since dawn. We will continue to keep you updated." Nubins face collapsed with despair.

He feared it may be the end and was worried desperately for his family.

The producers signaled to Peter, "And we're off." Peter just sat there.

He looked up at his producer and wanted answers. "Why is it that no one knows what the hell is going on out there?" Peter asked as he removed his ear piece and microphone.

"Prime Minister Sherrod is holding an emergency press conference in half an hour," the Producer offered half heartedly. "We will know more then." It was his only advice.

Peter Nubins had been doing this too long to be kept in the dark. "If there is something you know, that I don't, you should have let me in on it before!" Peter demanded an answer.

"Before what?" His producer asked.

Nubins shook his head. "Before I went on the air." Peter said and went over the papers an assistant handed to him.

"Look, its purely speculation at this point," the producer told him. "But everyone that has called in says these killers are inhumane monsters, and have never seen anything like it before." He continued. "They are breaking into the houses or just setting them on fire. But we have to wait to see what the MAN says. Give it half of an hour." The producers speculation intrigued Peter on many levels.

"Half an hour might be too late." Peter Nubins mumbled to himself.

CHAPTER SEVENTEEN

"Beginning Of The End"

"Time and tide wait for no man."
- Geoffrey Chaucer

An elaborate abandon subway station underground set the site for the North American starting point.

Situated on a loop of track in front of City Hall, it was the original southern terminal of the Inter borough Rapid Transit subway. It was very similar to the one Cyrus utilized before to rally his troops and was a perfect setup seeing that this station had been closed for over sixty years, and was abandon by all human activity. This station was much larger than the previous with tunnels that lead to the surface. Over a hundred vampires gathered around a makeshift podium and listened to Cyrus speak. Directly next to him was

Nephtali and two more of his faithful and most dominant aides. "Brothers and sisters, followers of Julian," he began. "Our kind has begun to fill the world's human population with fear, and now we will get to watch as their fears are extinguished along with their lives!" Cyrus leadership was working to full effect.

Nephtali nudged him. "They've heard it all before Cyrus. Just let them loose," he prodded. "That's all we have left to do."

Nephtali was right. Suddenly there was an interruption, but only to Cyrus' attention. The sound of a metal pipe falling somewhere in the vicinity. He paused only a moment. "Malivick." Cyrus uttered to himself. He knew that his brother was watching.

Nephtali was stunned as a silver arrow shot out of the darkness and pierced straight through the chest of Zip, one of the top aides that stood next to him. "Oh Shit!" Nephtali shouted in surprise. Zip dropped to his knees and gasped for oxygen. Cyrus leaned over to examine him, as his ally fell backward, dead.

"It's Malivick," Cyrus told the others. "Find him!" Three of his top henchman descended into the darkness of the tracks far back in the tunnel.

The three followed their nocturnal instincts and scanned the darkness for a heat signature. "Come on. Over here!" One of the vampire got a hit. They searched inside an old train car that was rusted and covered in webs and soot. One of the vampire fired off numerous rounds from his German SMG MP40, and smashed out every window in attempt to kill their target.

Out of the darkness, Malivick leaped from on top of the train. He slid down to the edge and kicked two of the vampires off of the sidewalk down a four foot fall onto the tracks. Simultaneously another silver arrow assassinated one of the attackers.

Malivick unleashed his fury on the vampire closest to him first with a combination of lethal punches and kicks. He disarmed the machine gun wielding vampire, and quickly grabbed the gun. Malivick finished the vampire off with multiple shots from the SMG.

Malivick avoided attack from the second of Cyrus' followers and ducked behind the wall of the train car as the vampires unloaded round after round at him. Malivick dropped the dispensed MP40 sub machine gun and pulled out a pair of semi automatic pistols as several more vampires joined the fight.

"*Great.*" Malivick didn't like the odds.

Cyrus was frustrated by his brothers interference. He wanted him eliminated now. "Take care of him for good, Andirion." Cyrus said. "The rest of you let's go, no more waiting!" Cyrus led the following of vampires to the surface. The war in North America was about to begin.

Meanwhile, Malivick faced odds of twelve to one. Things were not looking good. He could hear Cyrus yell the final words before disappearing at the top of the station. "Leave no one alive! The time is now!"

Malivick knew he had to catch up with Cyrus, his current situation was getting out of control. He swung the samurai sword out of its case that hung around his torso and sliced through one of the vampires. The dead vamp hit the ground with a thud. Malivick flipped over two others and dodged a few shots that allowed him to escape certain death. There were just too many of them. The vampires regained the upper hand and continued to beat the bloody warrior into the ground. They were doing more to humiliate him than they were to actually kill him.

Suddenly, somewhere deep in the darkness of the tunnels Malivick's attackers were interrupted by a voice that penetrated through the subway tunnel. The echoes frightened Cyrus' fighters.

"There are other factors in play here, and your time has come." The raspy voice laid it out for the vampires.

Cyrus' men were furious. "Show your face and we'll see about that!" Andirion, the leader demanded as he fired off random shots into the darkness.

Six tribal vampires cloaked in shredded cloth, emerged from the tunnels. Judging by the smell they must have been residents of the underground station. The group took aim at Cyrus' fighters as Malivick slowly pulled himself to his feet during the fiasco and continued to fight off the evil vampires.

Closer to the surface in the subway system Cyrus led the pack up the tunnel to the surface as dusk began to set in. "Faster! Keep moving!" Cyrus noticed a connection to a newer part of the subway system, not on his schematics. He motioned for his crew to follow.

They approached the next subway station filled with people, many on their way home from work. Some passengers began to notice the large group of oddly dressed and out of place vampires. The weapons were a dead give away. "This is it," Cyrus concluded. "Bring our father home! Take this station and move up the tunnel to the surface and take the city!" His words ignited the vampires into a monstrous rage. It took only a minute for the vampires to murder every human in the station.

At the surface in the bustling New York City streets at dusk, dozens more vampires stood by and awaited Cyrus' signal. Moments later Cyrus emerged from the underground subway system followed by hundreds of weapon toting vampires. The two groups combined forces as the annihilation began.

Screams of horror and deathly pain rang through the night air. The vampires used specially created cannon-balls that exploded and caught fire on impact, burning the impacted structure to the ground.

Within minutes, as the fighting continued to grow, a helicopter from the local news arrived on the scene. Vampires scattered into homes and buildings and began dragging out crying families and with absolutely no remorse, ripped their bodies to threads. The humans were being killed by any method of the murderers choice.

A fight flared up between vampires and a swarm of New York State Police Officers that had just arrived on the scene. They captured four of the vampires and it seemed that they made the apprehension, but more vampires quickly ran to their rescue.

They decimated the authorities with ease then decided to flip their patrol cars for the hell of it. The vampires continued to kill more civilians as they moved on through the desperate city streets.

The cops that were killed by direct contact with vampires had now come back as vampire themselves, and they too joined in the attack. At that moment one soldier vamp took aim at the news chopper with a Rocket Propelled Grenade Launcher. The devastating explosion tore a hole through the side of Trump Tower and blew out half a dozen floors. The chopper fell in flaming pieces to the earth as more screams echoed in the night.

Malivick was still underground and continued putting up a good fight along side his mysterious new allies. Two of them were on the ground, dead next to two bodies of Cyrus's loyal following. He heard the explosion above him and expected the worst. He fought his way up the ladder back into the empty subway station.

The leader of the tribal vampires yelled to Malivick without turning away from his opponents. "Where are you going?" The vampire needed help to defeat the elite guards.

"I have to stop my brother!" Malivick yelled and turned back to the surface. "I have to go." He continued up the stairs without hesitation as the tribal vampires continued the fight in his place.

Malivick reached the surface and followed the path of destruction that led out the subway station and down the blood filled streets. He realized the war had begun and the end was imminent. Malivick had a nervous feeling, as if being followed, but disregarded his instincts as he moved more quickly in the direction of the screams. Sporadic population of the immediate area allowed the killing to spread even faster to the more densely populated parts of the city. Malivick arrived to a street corner where the police made their stand in a blockade effort. He put the scene together in his mind and realized he had been tricked.

Four vampires abruptly lunged at Malivick from behind the burning fire truck. He fought back and kicked one of them in the face, then dove at the others. Malivick grabbed one by the head and broke his neck, killing him instantly. Malivick jumped up then knocked the other two to their knees with little effort.

But from a inside nearby burning building four more vampires emerged, led by Kole. They all wielded automatic rifles and aimed them directly at Malivick. Cyrus appeared from the back of the group.

"You made it too easy, Malivick." Cyrus said as he paced in front of his lowered nemesis. Malivick attempted to produce a scheme that would take on all of them, but with the emergence of two more armed vampires, he quickly knew that he had no way out.

Malivick was forced to surrender to avoid being immediately dismembered. But his capture meant death soon enough anyway. Three vampires grabbed Malivick, the largest one kicked him in the back.

"Get him up!" Cyrus shot a sadistic grin at Malivick as the vampire he kicked in the face returned the favor with a roundhouse to the jaw.

From below, the tribal vampire sprung up and appeared behind Cyrus. He kicked Cyrus' legs out from under him and knocked him to his knees. "Let him go!" The tribal vampire yelled to the hostiles. He wanted to bargain one brothers life for the other. The tribal vampire pulled out his pistol and held it to Cyrus' head. It had become a volatile standoff. "So now what!?" The tribal vampire shouted. "Let Malivick go, and you can have this piece of shit back." The tribal vampire held Cyrus by his hair and shook him around.

Malivick fought free to relay the importance of Cyrus' death. "No. Kill him!" Malivick yelled.

"But you have to live," the tribal vampire told Malivick. "It doesn't end like this."

"What?" Malivick shouted. "You don't know what you're talking about, pull the trigger!" He was interrupted by a punishing kick in the back by Kole.

"Shut up!" Kole yelled as Malivick fell on his face. Kole put his foot on Malivick's back and stuck the gun to his temple. Malivick's eyes filled with rage. His power had increased through anger, a vampire inherited trait. "Let him go." Kole said.

"Not a chance." The tribal vampire wasn't buying.
He looked deep into Malivick's eyes and searched for any type of sign. He cocked the hammer back and pushed the gun further into Cyrus' face.

Kole just laughed. Suddenly, at scorching speed Cyrus slid around and took the gun from his captor. Cyrus knocked him to his knees and took aim at the tribal vampire. He smiled at his brother, then pulled the trigger twice. The tribal vampire was killed instantaneously. At the same time Malivick flipped over to his back, kicked Kole's arm and caused him to fire a few wild rounds. Cyrus dodged the erratic shots while Malivick kicked Kole's leg. His left femur gruesomely fractured in two. Malivick jumped and landed a spectacularly complex double kick on the second vampire while he moved away from the confrontation. "I'm sorry," Cyrus said laughing. "Did I kill your friend?" Cyrus took a few shots in his brothers direction, but Malivick was able to avoid the gunfire while he fought off five vampires with the gun that he grabbed from Kole.

Cyrus approached his brother timidly as the fight continued. Malivick was outnumbered five to one, but slow and steady he was able to counter the attack and fired off several rounds that struck four of the five vampires. Malivick was able to do this all while backing away from Cyrus. Malivick dropped the hammer of the gun again, but his ammo was spent.

Shit!

A grungy vampire with stringy long hair hammered Malivick with his monstrous forearm. The vampire thrust his jagged spear at Malivick, but he was able to dodge the nearly fatal attack and kick his opponent away. Malivick performed a kip up, then struck the vampire with a disarming kick. He then pulled out a pistol from one of the downed vampires and fired five shots through the vampire's heart. He turned to where Cyrus was standing, but he was gone. Malivick didn't waste a second and grabbed some of the weapons that were scattered around. He reloaded his gun, looked at the dead tribal vampire, then took off after his brother.

Ryan C. Stith

CHAPTER EIGHTTEEN

"Losing Faith Part One"

"We will require a substantially new manner of
thinking if mankind is to survive."
- Albert Einstein

The rising sun casted summer rays down upon a small village just East of Lisbon, Portugal. Low rise office buildings sat adjacent to a five story parking garage. A market filled with business owners and suitors of miscellaneous articles was organized below the parking structure.

Off to the west was a forested area that led to Lisbon and to the east was a single lane road to a larger, nearby city. Suddenly people began to appear running from the forest. They ran through the road and fled in to the shops. More and more people scattered into the market running in fear of their pursuing attackers.

Inside the second floor fire escape of the parking garage was pounding on the concrete as someone approached from the stairwell. The unseen figure pulled and pounded the opposite side of the locked door. Finally, as the door swung open Adrian rushed in. He looked down from the rooftop of the parking garage just above the market. Cassandra hurried in right behind him and hopped down onto the roof of the market. They scurried across a scaffolding to reach a service ladder on the side that led directly to the highest part of roof-top.

Just a few miles away Gray and Damian were using the inside of the local hospital as a staging area, while the German Military took aim outside. The military force had deployed two armored units, and numerous infantry soldiers were lined up and threatened to fire on their own people inside in order to stop the resistance.

"We have to do something, now!" Damian yelled to Gray. He measured his tone but stood firm.

H. R. Gray didn't seem as worried. "They're not gonna fire on their own," he told Damian. "Just be patient." Behind the two leaders were two dozen more vampires all huddled inside the front entrance of the hospital.

An older Doctor appeared from inside the hospital and made his way over to Gray. "I got the code, and unlocked the door to the underground tunnel." The doctor told Gray. "It will lead us to the woods about a mile down the road." The doctors eyes glowed red in the tungsten light of the hallway.

Gray took the good news in stride. "Great! Damian. Move out!" The vampire doctor led the large group down through a trap door and in to a long cylindrical tunnel. They jumped down one by one. Gray, Damian, and the vampire Doctor moved quickly down the tunnel as the other vampires followed.

The vampire doctor pulled out a timer and approached Damian. "I took the liberty of wiring all the floors with plastics." The doctor told him.

"What? How long do we have?" Damian asked feeling the urge to run.

The doctor looked down at the remote timer. "Thirty seconds," he looked back up to see Damian and Gray were already running to safety.

"Move! Faster!" Gray yelled for the group to get to safety.

The Lisbon military and Peace Patrol of Portugal prepared to enter the hostile infiltrated hospital. The leader of the human resistance commanded the fleet to the narrow passage. "Bravo, move in through the south entrance," the commander ordered. "We will flank from the rear." The military commanders wireless radio sent his orders to the entire fleet.

Infantry patrols moved into position with shields and other anti-riot gear. One soldier threw a concussion grenade into the front of the hospital entrance and moved in. Just as the final infantry soldiers relocated in to the entrance, explosives began detonating on each level. All three floors collapsed on top of hundreds of civilians and military personnel. The explosion filled the atmosphere for miles as the fire spread to the unarmored vehicles closest to the hospital. The military commander turned from the explosion and saw two dozen of the fiercest vampires loaded with RPG's and Anti Aircraft Missiles.

"FIRE AT WILL!" The commander yelled as he took cover. He watched on as his troops laid down heavy suppression fire.

The vampires wasted no time as they quickly eliminated the few remaining infantry soldiers, and then with two strategically placed shots of rocket fire they decimated the lead armored vehicle. Another rocket propelled grenade whizzed by and hit the largest of the armored units directly in the fuel tank. The impact caused yet another extraordinary explosion that sent the tank twenty meters into the air. It flipped and landed upside down on top of the remaining human opposition in the area.

Adrian and Cassandra could see the explosion from their location.

"They're getting close." Adrian tossed Cassandra a solid black case and unpacked his rifle. The sniper rifles were quite stunning at first sight. They had a modern look but utilized highly advanced technology for upgraded accuracy and range. They checked the digital calibrations, took count of ammo, and loaded up.

Gray and Damian followed by dozens of others emerged from a large circular tunnel made to resemble a drainage pump. The vampires sliced through the people that hid in the heavily forested area just west of where Adrian and Cassandra were located.

"So where do we go from here." Damian asked Gray. "That really slowed us down." He consulted the PDA for further detailed instructions.

Gray looked into the forest and in the far off distance could see camouflaged movement. "We cut straight through." Gray replied without mincing words. Damian followed close behind as he charged off through the woods.

"Let's go!" Damian repeated Gray's act and the band of vampires moved through the forest closer to the resistance.

THE NEXT PROJECT

Nagpur, Maharashtra, India

High above sea level in the mountainous region of Central India, Roth along with over three hundred vampires rushed through villages and mutilated the innocent without a second thought. Roth consulted his PDA and began to input the status of his movement when the sunlight became shadowed as darkness swept over the area. "What the?" He looked into the sky and saw the sun eclipsed by a red halo that other than the color resembled the moon. With very little light he went back to his PDA. Roth finished up then caught up with the middle part of the group as they came upon a narrow river.

"Keep moving!" Roth moved further to the front of the group and was ready to strike what would be the largest village yet. The vampires moved across the narrow bridge slowly, patiently and had to wait for others to cross. Roth reached the opposite side of the bridge, but oddly enough the capital city of Nepal seemed completely deserted. Just for good measure Roth instructed the vampires to destroy any structures that stood. Dozens of the vampires shot fire charged arrows into the frail homes made of material that was mostly flammable. The large vampire following continued to file across the bridge as a thunderous rumble trembled the ground beneath the vampires.

Hundreds of villagers charged from a bunker dug behind the bridge. The humans wielded swords, bow and arrows, and a few even from rebel militias had guns. At first the vampires were taken aback with surprise. Even Roth hesitated.

The citizens charged straight for the large gathering of vampires. The front lines collided and a bloody battle ensued. Roth sliced through a human abdomen with his axe and cleared a path with a few more swings. As he moved through he kicked one opponent in the face as he almost got walloped by a large stick. Roth decapitated the man and laughed. "Your kidding. Your going to kill me with a stick!?" Roth flinched and gasped for oxygen. He reached and touched his back and right shoulder and felt the arrow that had just pierced his flesh. He dropped to his knees and writhed in pain as the human stood in front of him and watched as Roth reached back around and pulled the arrow from his shoulder just beneath his collarbone. He spit blood from his mouth and smiled. Behind the human, a vicious vampire appeared to save the day, with a clumsy swing of his broad sword he decapitated the human victim.

Another adversary charged at Roth, but he readied the bloodied arrow and jammed it right through his neck. Seemingly, the humans were outnumbered and the power of the vampires soon showed. The size of the human force was cut in half in minutes.

THE NEXT PROJECT

Panorama, Brazil

Hidden by the darkness, Eva knelt behind a boulder in the Mato Grosso region of Brazil just about to attack a small village. She was in mid communication on her radio. "That's right. Hundreds more showed up, and now we're two thousand strong." Eva transmitted across the South American continent and the Gulf of Mexico to Cyrus in the northeastern United States. "After we crossed the Brazilian border from Paraguay I sent half of them to the northwest and I am leading the others through Brazil." Eva made sure she was in the clear. "Well right now we are refueling the convoy and gathering more ammunition and then we are moving in on another city." She motioned for the group to gather around. "Yes I do remember what you said, but." Cyrus didn't even let her finish. "Alright." Eva ended the radio communication. She moved down the hillside to the convoy of vampires.

"Alright so we have to move out now." Eva tells the others. A muscular Brazilian vampire turned to Eva.

"We need more time to recoup before we move in." He told her. "This region has a strong militia force that will be waiting for us." Eva nodded, but knew she had to follow her orders.

"Cyrus says we gotta go, we gotta go." Eva rendered. "Bayless, tell the others, and let's move out." Eva readied her weapons and the troops began to file out.

"You got it." Bayless moved to the armored vehicles and gathered the other vampires. They resupplied grabbing extra ammunition before hurrying up the hillside.

Colin along with around eighty militia fighters hid in the darkness of a large cathedral over the hillside near Panorama. They each wielded a rifle and pistol among other weapons as they awaited the vampires attack. Colin slipped a cigarette in his mouth and lit it. "So we wait until they enter the village and go to work, that's when we surprise them. We can expect a few hundred, so I hope your men are ready for a fight Joe." Colin said as he took a long drag on the cigarette.

"This is what we do!" Joe shouted. "Don't worry about us, just make sure you find the leader and kill him." The leader of the militia understood his mission.

"That's what I do." Colin took his place back at the window. He looked up over the hillside, and at that very moment there was a massive explosion outside that destroyed a near by building.

More explosions followed and soon after, heavy small arms fire was heard. The vampires were marching down the hillside and setting the buildings ablaze. "Shit! They're burning the buildings." Colin said alerting the others. "Get ready we may have to move out early."

Back outside the cathedral, villagers emerged from their burning homes, screaming as they met their doom. These particular vampires were reborn from dead humans that were bitten by the creatures. They were much more aggressive and went straight for blood. So not only were the vampires using guns and other weapons, but the reborns were aiding the war by seeking out and ripping apart any living humans flesh, and they enjoyed every plasma extracting second of it.

Eva emerged from the flock of attacking vampires. "Burn the church!" She screamed to the others as she adjusted the assault rifle strapped around her shoulder. Only seconds later an RPG was fired into the church and caused another intense explosion. The destruction filled the sky with dust, debris, and smoke. The air became difficult to breathe, which as bad as it is, was the least of any living humans worries.

The night sky was lit up from the fire, and created a dangerously catastrophic battle field. Most villagers were attempting to flee even though they had no idea what they were up against. However, their efforts were quickly extinguished by the vicious vampire uprising.

Colin grabbed his trusty M-16/203 from the weapons cache and checked to make sure it was ready as his cigarette burned down to the filter. "It's time. Move out!" Colin led the militia as they busted through the burning entrance of the cathedral and moved into the village.

The humans laid down heavy gun fire as the initial battle got underway. Colin strategically took cover while popping off round after round, and brought vampire after vampire to their death.

Eva turned to the opposition and with cat like quickness moved in with her short swords slicing and dicing through three of the militia simultaneously. Crouched behind the fire lit barrels Colin watched as Eva sneaked up on the leader of the militia unsuspectingly. Colin quickly moved into action.

Two vampires dove over the barrels with fury in their eyes. They double teamed Colin and he was easily disarmed. Colin's gun slid across the pavement as they continued to beat on him. During the commotion he was able to trip up one vampire from his knees. Colin jumped up and pulled down on the vampire breaking his legs, and without missing a beat he lunged at his next attacker. Colin grabbed his opponent's sword and sliced him open. The vampire fell to the dirt gushing blood from his torso.

Colin finally got to his feet and moved in on Eva. Militia Joe saw Colin running toward him and moved out of the way just in time to avoid being sliced to pieces by Eva's dazzling short swords. Colin pulled out his samurai sword and took a swipe at Eva, but she ducked away, and that sparked the beginning of the battle.

They circled around an old sedan that was the target of rocket fire, it crackled from inside the charred remains as fire crept up to available oxygen. Bayless saw the fight and interfered with a high kick to Colin's throat. Two shots from Colin's assault rifle rang out and Bayless collapsed to the ground, dead.

Eva was too fast for Colin and she knocked the gun and the sword from his hand, threw him down, and climbed on top of him. "You should have stayed in bed gringo!" she yelled in Colin's face. "You have no chance." Eva choked him out with the dull side of the blade. After a few moments without oxygen Colin started fading out of consciousness. Colin mustered one final wind and kicked Eva off of him. He sat up gasping for air.

CHAPTER NINETEEN

"Evil Falters"

"If you don't risk anything.
You risk even more."
- Erica Jong

Cassandra set the rifle against the side of the wall and peered down to the street checking her line of fire. She took a quick look around the area. They were at one of the highest points in the vicinity.

"I'm going to take the rooftop across the street. That's a good place to set up the other rifle." Adrian brushed the hair out of

Cassandra's face and looked into her eyes searching for any shred of doubt. "Are you sure your ready?"

There was not a trace of fear upon the gaze of Cassandra. "I'll be fine Adrian," she responded. "We have to do this," there was a pause as another explosion shook the parking garage somewhere in the distance. "Did you hear that?" Cassandra asked.

"They're close." Adrian gave Cassandra a kiss, slid the rifle around his shoulder, and headed off down the ladder as the sound of screams and sirens grew closer.

Just a few hundred yards away from the parking garage, a large group of vampires began moving into an area filled with homes and small shops. The path led to the market square.

Damian and H. R. Gray were near the middle of the pack catching the humans as they fled from their burning homes. Damian grabbed one of them but the human pulled away and ran. "Stop running you coward!" Damian jolted. "Stay still so I can kill you!" Damian gave chase after he ripped a street sign from the concrete. He jumped onto the roof of a car and dove fifteen feet into the air. He spun on the way down and killed three humans with the steel pole.

Gray just smirked. "Much easier than I thought," he said to himself. Suddenly the sirens erupted even closer to the assault.

Humans scattered out through the village without a clue as to where they should go. Their only natural instinct was to panic. Mass chaos reigned across the lands.

A small task force of local police emerged from a burning building. Gray stopped the attempted attack, "Damian! Behind you!" He yelled out.

Damian whipped around and smashed two police officers with the steel sign, just as they were about to attack. The officers flew head first into a nearby burning car. Damian and another vampire proceeded to murder several more police officers with their own guns.

Gray side kicked one officer and nailed the other with a roundhouse. Damian finished them both after he pierced the steel through their sternum.

Damian looked around in satisfaction as he realized that they had wiped out an entire police squad.

Cassandra watched as Adrian climbed the service ladder on the side of the building. When he reached the top he pulled the ladder up. Adrian set up the tripod and rifle. He readied more ammunition, glanced at Cassandra, then looked through the scope.

Adrian examined the distant streets where sporadicly humans tried to get inside buildings and to safety. More and more humans passed by him and soon began to flood the area. The vampires appeared not far behind, as they continued to rip apart every human being without mercy. Adrian pulled away from the scope. He freaked for a second, but they were still hundred of meters away. He pulled the mouthpiece of the radio up to speak. "I see them. They're coming."

Adrian stared at Cassandra. "To the end Adrian." Cassandra said as she tried to enjoy that last moment with Adrian.

"To the end," Adrian was confident they would see each other again. He once again looked through the scope to line up his shot.

"Don't shoot until they reach the market." Adrian followed his first target through the street as he moved closer. He took a quick moment to himself, somewhat disillusioned.

The first shot was fired.

Neither Damian nor Gray heard the shots in all of the commotion. More rounds were fired and this time Gray watched two front line vampires go down. "What was that?" He said turning to Damian.

"Over there!" Damian pointed to the rooftop where Cassandra was shooting from as more vampires collapsed to the concrete, dead.

Cassandra switched from using the scope to pick off the closer vampires, one by one. The bodies began to pile up and quickly reached dozens of dead vampires.

"They're getting too close!" Cassandra shouted over the radio. "Shoot faster!"

On the adjacent rooftop Adrian opened up fire on the vampires without missing a shot. He looked through the scope and watched a horrible and dramatic transformation. The fateful generals Damian and Gray sprouted enormous black wings. If hell was real they were straight from the depths of the deepest pits of hell. Adrian watched on as the two took flight high out of sight. But he didn't stop shooting. He continued to fire at the dozens of vampires that were nearing his position.

A deafening thud crashed down behind him, when he turned around he was whipped hard with a pistol held by the demonic H.R.

Gray. Adrian fell down bumping the sniper off the roof and down to the ground twenty feet below.

Gray hovered over Adrian meanwhile Cassandra looked up to see her worst nightmare. Without missing a beat she turned, took aim, and fired a single round from the rifle that was dead on. Small pellets ripped through the flesh of H. R. Gray and he collapsed to the ground.

Damian landed on the rooftop behind Cassandra and startled her, but without hesitation fired two shots. Time seemed to stand still as Damian nonchalantly sidestepped both rounds of gunfire. Cassandra was stunned. The two stood face to face as Adrian struggled to his feet.

Damian delivered a deadly forearm shiver to Cassandra's head that disarmed and put her to the ground. Adrian picked up Gray's gun and turned to fire, but Damian jumped behind a steel air conditioning structure on the roof just in time.

"Shit!" Adrian yelled. "Cassandra!" He feared the worst. He went to the edge of the rooftop, looked down, and saw the vampires had surrounded the building and set it on fire. He took two shots with his pistol and killed a couple more transformed vampires. He pushed the ladder down, but more vampires intercepted so he quickly pulled it back up.

Adrian needed an exit strategy, and quick. He hustled to the opposite side of the roof, took a deep breath, and started running to the edge of the rooftop. Adrian leaped about twenty feet out and crashed down on the roof of a car.

He was instantly surrounded by four blood thirsty vampires. One of them grabbed Adrian's arm as he landed, but he pulled the vampire on top of the car and used him as a shield. Another vampire next to the car took aim and fired at Adrian, but hit the other vampire instead.

Adrian threw his dead vamp shield down onto the attacking vampires. He dropped down, swept his leg around, and double kicked the other two zombie like creatures. Adrian was still being shot at, but he evened the score by pulling the vampires head through the window. Adrian grabbed the disabled vampire's gun and flipped over the roof, fired two shots, and killed him. He entered the street with both guns, and shot his way into the parking structure toward Cassandra. Adrian appeared in the doorway, and reloaded as he headed for the side of the building where the service ladder was located. He climbed to the roof and saw Cassandra on the ground motionless and bloodied. "Cassandra!" Adrian shouted and immediately moved toward her. Damian emerged from behind a steel air conditioning unit, and surprised Adrian with a clothesline from his enormous bicep. Adrian was stopped in his tracks. Damian picked him up by the neck and held him easily over his head. Then, Damian rushed the steel framed mechanism and Adrian's head smashed through it, sparks flew out, and caused a small fire to ignite in the wiring of the box. The tip of an iron rod glowed bright orange in the fire as Adrian watched from his back as Damian grabbed the iron and approached. Damian held the burning hot iron core to Adrian's face.

Adrian grabbed at it in attempt to push it away but Damian thrust it further into his face and burned him severely. Adrian screamed in pain, but Damian just laughed as Adrian's flesh sizzled on the tip of the iron prod. Damian pulled it back almost as a tease and prepared to impale Adrian. He hovered over him about to strike.

Then a single gunshot was fired.

Pellets pierced Damian's chest, directly through his heart. His flesh and spinal cord collapsed over. Damian's body fell to the ground, and Cassandra stood above him as smoke billowed from the barrel of her gun. She reloaded and started to pick off the vampires again. Adrian took a deep breath and got to his feet and picked up his weapon. Just as he was about to check on Cassandra, two vampires appeared from the ladder. Adrian turned and with two shots killed both of them.

Air raid sirens sounded in the distance as Adrian looked over the edge of the building to see about twenty more vampires that were moving to their location. "Come on. We're not safe here anymore." Adrian said. "We have to go." Cassandra continued to fire round after round at the enemy. "Cassandra. Let's go!" He shouted. She finally pulled back and they slid down the ladder to the third floor. They moved to the stairwell, but paused when footsteps approached. Adrian pulled the pin from a grenade and tossed it down the stairwell.

The explosion killed four more vampire fighters. Adrian checked to make sure they were dead and then moved down to ground level.

The sound of a muffled German voice blared from a loud speaker somewhere nearby. The message repeated again, this time in English.

"Attention citizens! Your allied military needs your help!" The voice commanded. "Come out into the streets and fight for your freedom and fight for your life. Your military has taken control the majority of fighters, but we need help." The message repeated again, getting louder and closer.

In the streets of Lisbon, Adrian and Cassandra handled a few more vampires that rushed them from around the other side of the building. More gunshots were heard from around the same corner. "I'm almost out of ammo." Adrian gave Cassandra a desperate look.

"So am I," she replied with a sign of distinct anger.

Adrian fired off a few more rounds that put an end to the flood of vampires. Suddenly, the vehicle equipped with the PA device, blaring the message rolled around the corner. It's a decked out military style hummer with some advanced modifications. The infantry soldiers next to the vehicle surround Adrian and Cassandra.

Three German infantry soldiers pointed their weapons at the couple, but quickly realized that they were not hostile.

Adrian already feared that they would be mistaken for the enemy.

"Do you see any more of them?" The soldier asked as he looked around at all the dead vampires. "You sure did a lot of killing."

"No. None left." Cassandra gave a sure answer.

"You two did all this?" The second soldier was astonished. Cassandra and Adrian looked at each other.

"We, had a little help." Adrian explained.

The rebel's communications device relayed a detailed message in German to the leading rebel commander. "Well. The city is contained," the commander said, "return to your homes." The soldiers stood down and began to move out but Cassandra insisted further as she caught up to the soldiers.

"No. It's not over," she continued, "they won't give up like that." Cassandra offered the truth, but the soldiers didn't know what they were up against.

However now they were more suspicious of the pair. "Like what?" The commander asked. "They're all dead."

Adrian was careful of his choice of words. "This plague has spread to every shore stopping at no borders," he said. "It is not over."

"Yeah, well our fronts are in the clear," the soldier told them. "Now return to your homes!" Adrian took the offer, but with hesitation.

"Fine. But I'm telling you that this is -- " Adrian was interrupted when a vampire dove from the rooftop and landed on the Rebel Commander. The reborn vampire bit a hunk of flesh from the commanders throat and rendered him incapable of anything but dying.

One of the soldiers fired off several shots, but the vampire dodged all but one bullet that hit him in the leg.

The vampire grabbed the soldier's gun with ease and kicked him to the ground. He aimed the gun at the soldiers' head, but before anyone else could react Adrian fired two shots in to the vampire's chest. That put the hostile on the ground in a hurry. Adrian lowered his gun and approached the soldier.

The Rebel Commander was alive! He seemed to already have transformed into a vampire. The former soldier still bleeding from the throat fired his gun at Adrian. Adrian had to think quick, and made the most of his surroundings by grabbing the street sign used previously by Damian and swung in the line of fire and the shots ricocheted off into the air. Adrian threw the pole and hit the vampire soldier. The force sent him into the building that was already ablaze. Adrian found a spear on the ground and used it to stake him to the wall and watched as he burned to death.

Adrian and Cassandra turned back to the soldiers.

"You... You are one of them." The soldier told Adrian.

"No." Adrian replied. "Wait a minute... I just saved your life." Adrian was afraid he may not have been able to explain his way out of this one.

The rebel soldier shouted something in German and the other infantry soldiers surrounded the two. "You're part of all this." He said. "You are responsible!" Adrian and Cassandra looked at each other and knew their luck may have ran out.

Panorama, Brazil

The primal fight continued in the small village just outside Panorama. Multiple fires burned all around and the smoke clouded the atmosphere. In the center of it all was Eva and Colin who were still going at it. Colin had the upper hand as he had Eva backed against a wall. He choked the life from her, but then suddenly his expression changed from anger to pain after an arrow hit him square in the back. It was dug deep, far into his chest. Colin still continued to defend himself against Eva's onslaught which intensified as he lost massive amounts of blood.

"You, bitch!" Colin shouted. Eva smiled then kicked Colin in the stomach. It brought him to his knees.

"I told you." She said. "You should have stayed in bed. Too bad. You *were* kind of cute." With a swing of her two short swords she sliced Colin's head clean off. She wiped Colin's blood from her face, looked up to see Militia Joe, the leader of the humans in the village, and moved in for the kill. Things were not going well for the resistance.

Ryan C. Stith

Alverca do Ribatejo, Portugal

Adrian and Cassandra stood face to face with the rebel soldiers they had just saved. Even more soldiers linked up with them as they all surrounded the military Hummer. The leader of the unit approached the situation. More mumbling in German slang added to the volatile situation. The commander turned back to Adrian.

"On your knees," he demanded, "both of you." The soldier pulled out his side arm.

"We are not part of this." Cassandra persuaded. "We are against all that they are for. They want all humans *dead*."

The commander interrupted her. "I don't want to hear anymore!" he shouted. "On your knees! NOW!" The soldier grew impatient and moved in to speed things up.

"Don't do this." Adrian tried to reason with the soldier.

"Or what?", the Commanding Officer kicked Adrian which made him fall to his knees. Cassandra jumped at the soldier, but two other beastly uniformed men grabbed her.

"Get your hands off of her!" Adrian said with his final breath and jumped back to his feet toward Cassandra. The Commanding Officer aimed his M-16 rifle and fired two shots.

Both were direct hits to Adrian's skull. His lifeless body fell to the concrete. Cassandra pulled away from the soldiers and knelt by Adrian. She lifted his head as his eyes rolled back and she knew he was dead. Cassandra became hysterical and began sobbing. The soldiers all aimed their weapons at her.

149

"Kill me," she said, "just fucking shoot me!" Cassandra bowed over Adrian's body and continued to sob. The soldier looked at his Commander, and in an act of compassion lowered his pistol.

"Let's go." The commander ordered. "Second unit, move west and clear the area. We will continue into the city."

The infantry soldiers disappeared into the fog of war followed closely by the military commando vehicle. The soldiers fell in under new command.

Cassandra cried over Adrian's body as the tank rolled off, out of sight. She stood up and with tears in her eyes took a grenade from the dead soldier's pack. She pulled the pin and with all of her effort lobbed the grenade at the soldiers. The grenade hit the ground and rolled under the German military style Hummer. An awesome explosion followed and destroyed the commando vehicle and killed all inside. The soldiers that surrounded the vehicle also suffered fatal burns and one by one fell to the ground as rifle shots echoed out from within the mayhem.

Through the flames Cassandra stood weeping. She wiped her tears, reloaded her gun then disappeared into the disparaged village.

CHAPTER TWENTY

"A Global Crisis"

"Where there is no vision, the people perish."
- Holy Bible Proverbs 29:18

Air Force One flew despairingly low over the Eastern Coast of the United States. Inside the private United States government jet, Secretary of State Lamar Guthry observed damage on the ground through the window. Lamar was on the phone with the President of the United States of America.

"Mister President, I don't know how to explain the catastrophic damage I am seeing other than it is beyond anything, *anything* that I thought possible in such a short amount of time." Lamar sat back in his leather reclining seat. "It seems impossible how quickly and under the radar this attack came upon us."

The streets were empty. Dead bodies littered the area. Soon dozens of vampires could be seen feeding on the dead human bodies. "Sir, I know we have taken the stance that this is some kind of organized attack by worldwide terrorists, but this attacking force is inhuman like." He continued. "It is rapidly wiping out all local and regional law enforcement agencies. They are in eighteen different countries now." Air Force One soared over a barricade where police attempted to make a stand, but were brutally dismembered.

"You have to put a face on the enemy soon, Mister President. Yes, I understand that they may posses chemical weapons, but the military must get involved or we might be looking at hell on earth." The secretary was forced to look away from the horrid disaster. "The sooner the better sir. Yes sir, Mister President." Lamar Guthry hung up the cell phone, then pulled out a video camera, and recorded the damage from the window. His shock didn't seem to translate to the President so he was going to document the damage himself.

United States Top Secret Underground Headquarters

The President of the United States sat in front of a television camera. Four top associates and secret service guards were in the room close by. Five large television monitors were in front of the President with the top world leaders from, Europe, Asia, Africa, South America, and Australia.

"We are still examining the link that this could be some kind of chemical plague." The President said candidly to the leaders of the world.

Asian Ambassador Nicolee was not afraid to speak in the same tone. "What exactly are you examining?" Nicolee asked. "The fact that millions of our people have been killed in six continents in twenty four hours!? While your teams are *examining* the situation, your people are being slaughtered on the streets and in their homes. Have you even seen what is going on out there?" The Asian Ambassador's voice echoed through the room and left the President to decide what was best for the world.

"I am being briefed with the latest and best intelligence available." The President said.

"Mister President." Nicolee continued. "Death is at our doorstep. If we do not act now, I believe the survival of our people are at serious risk." He tried to convince the President that more forceful action was necessary. Another leader, German Chancellor Gore jumped in the discussion.

"Oh. Do you really think so?!" Gore retorted. "Of course they are at risk! What do you think this is all about?" The Chancellor paused

153

to gauge his audience. "My office just received a video tape of an interview set to air on emergency broadcast in half an hour." Chancellor Gore continued. "The man is a German historian that claims there is proof that our attackers are not our kind and they want death for all humans," he paused, "and so far his *proof* on this idea checks out on paper."

The African Ambassador interrupted, "What do you mean?" The Ambassador asked wanting to get his question in first.

Chancellor Gore retorted. "Well it's just like any religion really." Gore stated. "I'm talking religious scriptures passed on from the beginning of time. We have the bible, the Koran, they are all based on faith. You have faith in your god right Mister President?" Gore asked.

The President looked confused, but went along anyway. "Of Course. But what religion would call for such a massacre?" He asked. "I've never heard such a thing."

Before the President could finish his thought German Chancellor answered.

"...Vampires..." Gore said woefully. The leaders gasped in astonishment, and there was a brief pause. A look of confusion bled from the face of the President of the United States.

"Vampires?" The African Ambassador finally broke the silence.

The President of the United States was not impressed. "You're kidding," he said, "Vampires are not real. They don't exist!" The President's persistence invoked suspicion among the other leaders. "What is it with you people and your hocus pocus the truth is out there crap?" He asked the Chancellor. "I mean just the other day I got an E-mail from some lunatic about some kind of vampire new year. And they wanted it acknowledged as a national holiday." The President quipped in an attempt to lighten the mood. "Wait, was that you Gore?" The world leaders sat silently tuned to the President's words of wisdom. Or lack there of. "What?" The President asked. "Just roll the footage."

The interview began to play on the large projection screen above the President. The other leaders watched the feed as well. Alvin Hughes, a gray haired veteran news reporter introduced his subject Doctor Viktor Sosa with a brief montage of photos that highlighted Sosa's career milestones.

"In a desperate time, everyone is now seeking an answer to the plague that has taken a gripping turn for the worst." Alvin said. "Religious figures do not know what is going on, government officials haven't a clue. So who do we turn to for the answer? Many are turning to Doctor Viktor Sosa. A modern day philosopher and lecturer on the theory of evolution who claims to hold the key to what really is happening on our streets and in our homes. And now here is the interview I conducted earlier today with Doctor Viktor Sosa."

Another previously recorded tape began to play.

"Doctor Sosa there has been talk recently that a sudden emergence of the vampire race could be responsible for the terror that we have witnessed all over the world in the past two days." Alvin Hughes said. "Is this true?" He asked the question the world was looking for the answer to.

Viktor Sosa was a seemingly methodical figure, with his jet black hair and piercing black eyes. "Not could." He replied. "They *are* responsible. And not only is the brutality of the murders proof of their existence, but also proof that the sequence of events that was predicted over four thousand years ago in the first recorded vampire scriptures are playing out here on Earth turning the planet into a battlefield."

"So you say all this has been documented." Alvin said. "The killings, the motives, and more?" He tried to grasp the statement.

"To the date." Sosa replied simply.

Alvin Hughes still had a sense of disbelief. "It certainly is odd that we haven't heard of this sooner." His disdain was evident as a hard line skeptic.

"The original text of the scriptures, called the Avinale Cipacol was found only thirty six years ago." Sosa said. "Most of society does not accept vampires into their reality so to them they don't exist. But now they have come out from hiding." The puzzle pieces were beginning to fall into place.

"And what do they want?" Alvin asked. "Why are they doing what they are doing?" He asked the money question.

Doctor Sosa sat up even more seriously and leaned toward his interviewer. "The only way to understand what the vampires believe is to quote straight from the text of their belief." Viktor said as he pulled out a black book with gold jewels engraved on the cover. He opened the book to his mark and began to read. "For those who follow my ..." The tape froze mid frame.

The President of the United States put the remote on the desk and shook his head. "I can't sit here and listen to this garbage. Forward it past this mess. What is it you want us to see Chancellor?"

The tape forwarded past the scripture quoting and then continued to roll as Viktor Sosa paused.

"You cannot question what they believe." Sosa said. "And what they believe will destroy the Earth. Vampires are desperately connected to their god, Elias Julian. They have faith they can eliminate a curse placed on their race long ago by killing the human population off by more than eighty percent. They have a deadline that unless they meet will renew the curse and bind it for eternity." Viktor's exposition lingered as he took a deep breath and sat back. "By releasing the curse it would awaken their deity Elias Julian from the dead." Sosa continued. "He would enslave the remaining humans and the vampire race would control the Earth forever. The vampires also would no longer thirst for blood. The part of the curse that dwindled the number of vampires over the last thousands of years." Viktor explained it with elegance. Just as it was written.

Alvin tried to dispute Viktor's claim. "But, correct me if I am wrong," he hesitated, "Isn't that what makes a vampire different than us? Their severe need to consume blood?"

"It is one thing, but definitely not the only difference. Sosa said. "Think more in terms of a genetics mutation. Most attributes in a human are increased dramatically with vampires. Speed, awareness, and strength. The whole nine." Viktor almost cracked a smile. It fazed Alvin.

"So someone created the vampire in a tube?" Alvin asked, stunned by the depth which Viktor went into with his story.

"That would seem the natural explanation but no, vampires are a natural spawn from human." Viktor attempted to offer solace.

Alvin looked over his notes, and choked up. "So we should be taking this threat very seriously?" Alvin asked. Sosa once again leaned up in his seat to stress his earnestness.

"This has been a serious threat from the beginning, but no one wanted to believe in this, until now." Sosa continued. "Too late. Just the way it reads in their scripture." Viktor's chilling description resonated around the world as the war continued through the night and in the day on every continent. "They are very well organized and prepared for this and they already have taken our countries by storm," he continued, "I believe what I am told to believe, just like everyone before me." Viktor took a drink from a nearby glass of water.

The President paused the tape. Back in the room of leaders, the German Chancellor looked over his latest report.

"That's it really." Gore said. "I'm not trying to influence any of you one way or the other, but you have to at least indulge the fact that this could be true." No one said a word. The President had an apparent struggle somewhere within himself.

Asian Ambassador Nicolee chimed in, "Just got off the wire over sixty thousand dead in Tokyo in the last hour alone." He said. "It's growing."

The diplomatic leader from Africa interjected a solution. "What if we surround the infected and contain the areas?" The African Ambassador asked.

German Chancellor Gore had already thought of that. "There is no containment," he added, "It has already spread too far and they are gaining quite an army."

The President quieted the chatter to get his word in edge wise. "What do you mean an army?" He asked.

Gore seemed to have all the answers. "Well vampires are killing massive amounts of people using a variety of methods from swords to chain saws." Gore said. "Apparently, those are the lucky ones. Any human that is bitten by a vampire will within minutes fall into a comatose state, and reawaken as a vampire. Supposedly they will immediately thirst for blood and that would just increase the hostiles numbers while concentrating ours." The President slammed his hand on the desk in disbelief.

"That seems a little far fetched!" The President said as he stood to his feet.

"That's based on the guy you just heard." Gore said just trying to make the connection.

Nicolee finished reading over his report. "So sixty thousand people being murdered an hour on my streets!?" He shouted. The tension continued to rise between the world's leaders.

The President attempted to calm his counterparts with a solution. "I have already deployed two full units to the affected areas." The President said. "The first will dock just off the eastern coast of Georgetown, in Guyana, South America. The other is moving into position off the coast of Hainan, China." The President tried his best to save the peace.

"My question to you all is how do you believe these units would be best utilized?" He asked. "If these murderers are what you say they are Chancellor, then I am going to need a good game plan. You don't think I have a strategy, do you?"

"With all due respect, these murderers, vampires, whatever they are, have spread faster than wildfire and our military blockades have failed." Gore said.

The diplomat from Australia finally spoke up, desperate for help. "The attackers have breached security in our federal buildings. He said. "We are requiring immediate assistance to hold off the offensive."

The President felt the walls closing in. "How many of them?" The President asked.

"According to all estimates on the up side of twenty-one hundred." The Australian's voice seemed much more panicked.

"And you have no defenses!?" The President yelled. He couldn't believe it.

"Sir, I am saying there is not much left to defend." The Australian leader said. "Most of the continent is burning to the ground. Almost all of our population in the Northern Provinces has been wiped out." The Australian leader went off camera to consult with his people.

The German Chancellor was bewildered. "You have to do something now Mister President." Gore said.

The President's military advisor who stood just behind the President cleared his throat. "If we nuke the north it would kill off the attackers." He muttered. But the President just looked up blankly at his associate.

"You want to nuke our capitals now!?" The African Ambassador shouted. "This is madness." He was appalled by the thought.

Nicolee agreed that the idea that a nuclear response would be a terrible idea. "Yes, what do you think you are doing here?" Nicolee asked. "Bombing our cities with chemical weapons is not an option. We are with you. Something needs to be done now, but this is not that something."

German Chancellor Gore nodded his head in silence. Surely someone must support this idea. "At this point I think all guidelines are out the window." Gore said. "I agree, it is collateral damage that is necessary to restore control of what we have left."

The Australian feed faded in and out, then static replaced the visual of the Australian leader.

"What's going on?" The President asked. "We lost connection with Australia." He was afraid for his Australian friend.

"Not sure, They are working to bring it back up." A technical aide said while he restored power to the monitor. Still nothing.

The President held his head in his hands, and exhaled deeply, "As I was just about to say, this could be our only option." The President said.

"Alright, we got 'em back." The aide told the President. "Video is still down but we have them on radio." He jumped up and went back to his computer.

"What is the status Australia?" Nicolee asked.

Static and sirens were followed by the frantic voice of the Australian leader. "We are over run," he said, "our defenses have been overtaken. We just lost power and control of two nuclear reactors."

"What!?" The President jumped to his feet.

The President's top advising officer entered the compound. "Confirmed two nuclear reactor's have been activated." He alerted the leaders.

The President stood face to face with his advisor looking for a shred of good news. "What does this mean?" He asked.

"The reactor's are active," the aide continued, "any improvised explosive anywhere around it will cause catastrophic results." The advising officer saw the deep concern of the President.

"Nicolee what do you think now?" The President asked. "How are vampires taking our defenses away from us? We must act now!"

Radio communication with Australia failed again.

The President stood and faced away from the leaders and everyone in the room. He just stood there, looking down at the floor. Suddenly he turned around, wiped a tear from his eye, and gave his orders. "Gentleman the situation and my choices are clear." The President said. "My job as President of the United States is to defend my people at all cost. As commander and chief I am ordering the immediate bombing of all inflicted areas. World wide."

"I think that we should get a say in this!" The African Ambassador interjected his authority, but the President had his mind made up.

"As long as one vampire remains there will be a threat to this country." The President said. "I will do whatever I must to kill them all."

Asian Ambassador Nicolee tried to interrupt, but was cut off by the President's adviser. "We have the most advanced technology as you all know." The adviser stated. "We are equipped and ready for situations such as this. It will be the most precise and accurate campaign in military history." The adviser turned to the President.

He thought over his decision one last time, "Make the phone call." He ordered.

"Yes Mister President."

CHAPTER TWENTYONE

"Pleasurable Update"

It was a devastating sight on the streets of what was once Downtown Manhattan. On the corner of all the streets transformed vampires fed on the dead, while the vampire soldiers roamed the streets.

South of this area was where the most action was. A skyscraper burned inside from the ground up. On top of the roof thousands of feet in the air, were three humans huddled together, trapped in a terrible situation. They screamed out for help that they already knew wasn't there.

Further south across the New Jersey border, there were legions of vampires that marched unopposed through the streets and left only death and destruction in their wake.

But just two hundred yards ahead of them was a human military roadblock set up to halt the attackers progress. Hundreds of civilians also had joined the ranks to back the United States Army National Guard.

At the very tail end of the pack of vampires was their leader, Cyrus. Nephtali stood tall, next to him. He followed up on the statistics worldwide on the PDA. Seeton, another of Cyrus' top aides approached.

"We got something to show you Cyrus." Seeton said excitedly.

Cyrus observed the front lines as they reached one hundred feet from the road block. "Nephtali, they have reinforcements moving in now. Perhaps you should call for backup." Cyrus said. Nephtali made the call.

"Uhm, Cyrus. We have something." Seeton said again trying to alert Cyrus of his message.

"It can wait." Cyrus responded. "We're busy!" His words were final.

Seeton hesitated a moment. "It's your brother." That changed Cyrus' tune in a hurry.

"You know where he is?" Cyrus snapped at him. He got right in Seeton's face and stared him down.

Seeton felt uneasy, but proceeded. "Something like that." Seeton whistled and three vampires dragged Malivick around the corner. His legs and arms were bound by shackles. Blood poured from his nose and mouth. Cyrus' expression lit up.

The vampires front line collided with the human defenders and gunfire erupted. The vampires got some help as the transformed beasts attacked the humans and went straight for blood without showing an ounce of mercy.

Flashes lit up the sky amidst the fog of war and Malivick obviously wasn't in the best of spirits but he still somehow managed to kick free during the commotion. He made his escape but the steel that entangled him weighed down heavily.

A barrage of gunfire from the humans took out several vampires, but many had to reload simultaneously and lost ground as the frenzied vampires moved quickly to break the line.

Malivick continued to fight back against his captors regardless of whether he was restrained or not. Nephtali came back in as the battle raged through the front line, and Cyrus even got in on the killing. Nephtali kicked Malivick down to help the others recover. "Cyrus, there are five other groups of about six hundred each further south of the city." Nephtali said. "I will radio them for backup." He relayed the good news while he kept an eye on the bloody and beaten Malivick.

"We don't need backup!" Cyrus shouted as he fought his way to the front of the battle. The humans eliminated an impressive number of vampires; however, with almost a one for one return, every time a human was killed, a vampire dropped as well. Unfortunately for the humans many of them died from being bitten, and soon transformed into the enemy. The vampire army continued to multiply.

One of the military commanders in charge of the roadblock operation, noticed the ammunition situation. "We're running low on ammo!" He shouted to his captain. "Try to conserve!" They all knew that wasn't possible. The vampires continued to attack seemingly from every direction.

Cyrus emerged from the front of the battle after miraculously dodging two gunshots and then slicing the legs off of two humans with a single swing of his sharp blade.

Malivick pulled away from the captors as they were attacked, however his hope quickly faded as a lightning fast kick from Cyrus put him back into the arms of the three captors.

Gunfire had all but stopped and the fight succumbed to blades and biting. Only thirty or so humans remained alive and were surrounded by the vicious enemy.

Malivick faded in and out of consciousness from the brutal kick he had just received, and moments later when he regained his composure, it was a sight of pure deception and mayhem. The legion of vampire were marching again unopposed. Cyrus, Nephtali walked in front of Malivick as his captors dragged him along; Malivick jerked on the chains.

Cyrus laughed in disgust as the killing around him continued. "It's no use." Cyrus said. "You're weak and pathetic just like the humans. Maybe it's better off that I kill you now." Cyrus whipped around with an evil grin. His captors thought it was a brilliant idea.

"You should kill him now," one of them said, "This is a hassle dragging him along. He's better off dead." Cyrus looked at his accomplices in disgust.

"Silence!" Cyrus shouted. "We will take him with us." He had other plans for his all but dead brother.

"Sir, we understand your reasoning, but we think he will just slow us down." He replied. Cyrus grabbed the captor by the throat and choked him viciously.

"Do you understand the meaning of silence?" Cyrus snapped.

The captor did his best to mumble what he wanted to hear.

Cyrus released his grip. "Good. Now I said he was coming with us," he told them, "Elias Julian will have his way with this wretched traitor." Cyrus turned to face Nephtali.

"You know what you speak is untrue." Malivick shouted at his brother. "Why do you continue to poison minds with your lies?" Malivick's captor whipped his rifle around and nailed him in the skull.

Cyrus turned back to Malivick and grabbed him by the hair. "Keep your mouth shut or I will make sure you never speak again." Cyrus let go of his head, but Malivick's eyes remained dead set on Cyrus.

"If you continue on this path you will wipe out the existence of both races. Of all races." Malivick tried to break through.

Cyrus let loose with a mighty punch to the side of Malivick's face that put him down to his knees. "Keep your mouth shut!" He demanded of his brother.

Malivick still looked up into Cyrus' eyes. "Do the right thing Cyrus, stop the killing." He continued to plead his case.

Cyrus turned to the captors, removed his pistol from his holster and put it to Malivick's temple. Cyrus flicked the safety off and pulled down the hammer. Cyrus' fiery expression burned a hole into his brothers memory.

CHAPTER TWENTYTWO

"Losing Faith Part Two"

"If you have abandon one faith, do not abandon all
faith. There is always an alternative to the faith we
lose. Or is it the same faith under another mask?"
- Graham Greene

The President of United States sat alone on a studio set in front of a camera. Philip Walker, the Presidents top associate walked up and handed him a copy of the pre-written speech. He stepped behind the desk and plugged the President's microphone in. "Alright try it now mister President."

"Audio, check." The President adjusted the microphone clip on his tie and placed his American flag pin just below it. "I think," he hesitated, "I should tell them about the air strike. It's the right thing to do, don't you think?" The President was having second thoughts, but Philip Walker convinced him otherwise.

"We strongly recommend that you refrain sir." Philip said. "It will just incite more panic and fear." Walker tried to give him confidence.

The President shook his head in disappointment. "Would you guess we could possibly have any more fear or panic in our world than we do now?" The President's friendship with Philip ran back some thirty years, they've always seen eye to eye.

But not on that day.

"It's not my job to guess mister President." Walker responded. The two exchanged an intense stare down, that abruptly ended when Vice President Linda Hamilton entered the room.

"Mister President, bombers are arriving in the target vicinity." Linda told him. "They are conducting a fly over until all fighters are in place." The Vice President had a seat in the production room behind the cameras.

The producer gazed into the monitor and adjusted the camera's aperture. "You're on in thirty seconds mister President."

The President did one final read over of his notes. Half nervous and half comical the President looked to his aide. "I want to pray, but now..." He searched for the right words. "I find it difficult to know who to pray to," the President paused again briefly, "are we alone in this fight?"

"We may find out soon Mister President." Philip said as he joined Linda in the production room. "Very soon."

THE NEXT PROJECT

The President was alone in front of the lights, and about to tell the nation and the world the bad news.

"Ten seconds." The producer took his spot next to the camera. The President inhaled and exhaled a few desperate deep breaths. "Five, Four, Three, Two" A light on top of the camera beamed red as the President got his signal.

The President thought a moment before he spoke. Millions watched him sit silently. "My fellow Americans, on this morning this country's citizens like many others are in grave danger." The President broke the silence. "We are risking extinction as a race and as we run that risk, I come to you, The American People with a plan of action. A plan of action in order to ensure that mankind survives this vicious attack." He paused briefly. "We face an unfamiliar enemy, a new unseen opponent. I am here, steadfast and I promise to fight until the end for the safety of our existence." The President choked up, but fought back the tears. "As Commander and Chief I am obligated to make some very difficult decisions. Our special forces units are moving in on the enemy as I sit here now. They are side by side some of the worlds top military forces. We will lead the world into battle and lead our existence out the other side." The President glanced off screen for a moment as if looking for confirmation.

"Our military has begun operations to eliminate these foreign enemies." He continued. "In this time of hopelessness, I ask you to have hope. And I tell you at a time of evident crisis, to keep the will and faith to survive!" His words brought little comfort to those driven from their homes with little or no family remaining. They were lucky just to be alive. "We will win this war! Godspeed." The red light went dim and the President sighed deeply.

"You are off the air, Mister President." The private Producer powered off the studio lights.

Philip Walker stormed back into the room. "Sir, we have a problem." Philip was interrupted by yet another high ranking official that busted in to the room.

"Mister President, you have to leave now." The secret service official declared. "We just lost audio and visual with the fighters. You have to get to the bunker, sir." Multiple secret service agents entered the room to make safe passage for the President and Vice President.

"We lost contact with all of them?" The President asked, stupefied.

The agents rushed the President down the hall. "All of them." Philip said. "We are trying to get them back on line. But we have to go. Right now."

They navigated down the narrowly enclosed corridor, down a short flight of stairs, and finally they came to a stop in front of a large sealed door armed with even more secret service. They stepped on a platform that lowered about fifteen feet underground.

The President was led off of the platform and through two more sets of containment doors. They finally entered the main operations bunker. The underground layer was an extraordinary military bunker with operational facilities that were ready to process and communicate all military operations. The President was hurried into the war room of sorts. All the logistics needed to run a war and the country could be done from this room. The information nerve center was the target for the President.

He entered the war room and stood behind three technicians that were punching away at their keyboards. "Where are my fighters?" The President placed his hand on the computer technicians' shoulder, who was steady pounding away on the keyboard.

"No idea," he replied, "we were tracking them all just fine, and then one by one they started dropping off radar. We have not been able to raise any of them on the radio since." The technician didn't blink or look away from the screen.

The President feared the worst, "Are they all dead?" he asked. A loud beeping alerted the technician of an interception on the satellite. "What is that?" The President leaned in closely to the blinking computer screen.

"Wait! I'm tracking something on radar." The technician said. The radar expanded to the large projection screen on the wall above the President. "It looks like two of the jets we deployed to South America."

Another computer technician seated at a radio wave mapping station, pulled off his headphones. "I still can't raise radio communication." He looked at the other technicians for support.

The President sensed something was amiss. "Where are all the others?" He asked.

"I don't know but, wait..." The tech hesitated. "The jets are coming back to us." The technician couldn't figure it out. The Vice President huddled over yet another defense monitoring station, stood up to get the Presidents attention.

"Defense incoming reads we have two incoming large ballistic missiles!" Linda shouted. She now realized that her Vice Presidency was practically meaningless. The President's eyes glazed as his renewed energy ran dry.

"What?" The President asked woefully. "Issue an intercept, now!" He ordered. "Where are they coming from?" The techs crashed on their keyboards even more quickly than before, trying to gather as much information as possible.

"Our automatic defense system should have already issued the intercept." Linda told the President. He couldn't believe it. "Two, five hundred pound nuclear warheads launched fourteen minutes ago from Clao de Claud off the Eastern Australian coast will make impact with the western Alaskan coastline and central Mexico." The Vice President added.

The Presidents face writhed in horror. "Clao de Claud." He said stunned. "They're our bombs." He bowed his head in dishonor.

The technician didn't even want to reply, "I'm afraid so Mister President."

The President swallowed the lump in his throat and tried to think of a solution, any solution. "Scramble jets to detonate them over the ocean" He said. "Do it now!"

"There's no time." Linda replied. "We're looking at ten to twelve minutes to scramble jets to a safe enough distance." The leaders could not believe they would see the day the United States was overtaken.

The President looked on the verge of breakdown. "How long do we have?" He asked softly.

Again the technician had to give the world ending news. "Four minutes." He said as sirens sounded all around the room. Red flashing lights pulsed to the sirens scream.

"Are we going to be safe here?" The President asked for the slightest hope.

Vice President Linda Hamilton, a long time department of defense employee knew the schematics of the structure in and out. "Yes sir, The warheads should not immediately affect the Eastern portion of the United States." The Vice President's assuredness brought some calm to those in the room.

New Jersey, United States

The enormous coalition of both rabid and trained vampires maliciously coalesced the bludgeoned society in America. They had squelched their freedom and dismantled the population. Thousands of vampires marched in New Jersey alone, while millions more around the United States and across the globe did the same. The death parade was under way.

At the tail end of the vampire convoy Nephtali and Cyrus walked casually followed by the captors that dragged Malivick along behind them.

"Good news." Nephtali said examining the PDA. "I just heard we control all of Australia. It's just like you said. More and more vampires came from the underground and are joining in the fight."

Cyrus stopped suddenly and caused those behind him to halt. "WHAT?" Cyrus asked. "It's happened already?"

"What's happened already?" Nephtali was in the dark.

"The siege of Timor." Cyrus said as Nephtali just shrugged. Cyrus caught up to the group. He grabbed his communicator. "Fantastic! Lets keep moving, it's almost time to go home and see our father!" Nephtali half understood with a shrug and grin. Cyrus turned to his brother who was only half conscious. "You see Malivick," He taunted, "It's all coming to pass just like I knew it would." Cyrus gave his brother the most hateful look.

Sweat beaded down the Presidents forehead as he awaited impact of the nuclear weapons. Technicians were scurrying all around him searching for a way to save the union that had been built. The entire foundation was prepped for destruction.

"Approximately two minutes until impact." The technician alerted everyone of the impending attack.

The President's eyes were still trained on the radar, and awaited word from his jets. "Where are those fighters?" He asked. "Are they in position!?"

"They are in the air, but they are not showing up on radar." The technician explained.

Philip Walker had the latest intelligence on the estimated time. "They won't get there in time sir. I'm sorry." Philip said. The President clutched the desk he was sitting on. He held his breath in anxiety as did everyone else in the room.

"One minute." Counting down seemed useless. It only added to the anxiety.

The President searched for answers. "Is there anything I can do?" He asked. It seemed there was nothing left to be done.

CHAPTER TWENTYTHREE

"Two Days Later"

"All my possessions for a moment of time."
- Elizabeth I

Potsdam, East Germany

The light of Elias Julian burned brighter than ever in the east. To the west a small white dot appeared in the sky. It grew larger as the blinking lights approached. The object lowered and continued to grow as finally a Gulf Stream jet came in to view. It slid down onto an open plain and came to a stop.

The cockpit door opened and Cyrus immediately jumped out. He was followed by Nephtali, Malivick, and of course Malivick's captors. Before the last one exited, he tossed down two large duffel bags from the jet.

Nephtali opened one of the bags and pulled out an M-29 sub machine gun. Cyrus loaded up on guns and ammo before looking up into the sky. "Where the hell are we?" Cyrus asked. "This isn't where I told you to land."

"There was nowhere to put it down." Nephtali explained. "This is the closest I could get us. I tried to tell you."

Cyrus didn't care at that point. "Forget it," he replied smugly, "How far is Berlin?"

"About twenty-five kilometers. But," Nephtali was interrupted by a voice familiar to Malivick.

"Nice work Cyrus. You made it." the female voice said as she appeared from behind the Gulf Stream jetliner.

"It's good to see that you made the right choice, Cassandra." Cyrus replied. "For your sake." He congratulated her on a job well done.

"Yes well, I thought about what you said and you're right." Cassandra said. "The human race isn't worth saving." Behind them, Malivick jerked on his shackles with all his energy. Cyrus and Cassandra turned to Malivick and watched one of the captors pistol whip him.

Malivick dropped to one knee and writhed in pain. He didn't drop his head for a second, only stared into his brothers eyes.

"It's too bad Malivick." Cassandra said. "You should have listened to me. If you could just realize that it's better for you and I, if this happens. It would be so much easier with your help." Cassandra's deception had made hope anything but possible. She turned back to Cyrus and handed him a personal digital assistant. "Less than a click east from here is Potsdam. I have a ride waiting to take us to meet up with the others." Cassandra told them. Cyrus' boiling blood cooled.

"Good work." Cyrus said. "Let's move."

"Is someone going to stay and watch the jet?" Cassandra asked.

From the back Malivick spoke up. "You won't need it." Malivick spouted. "We're all going to die. Cyrus knows what will happen, but he just won't tell you."

Cyrus turned to pound on his brother, but before he could, Cassandra whipped around and stabbed Malivick in the leg with a broad dagger.

Malivick growled in pain and jerked tight on the chains connected to the restraint device. Cyrus grabbed Cassandra by the throat. "What do you think you are doing?" Cyrus asked.

"I'm sorry Cyrus." Cassandra said. "He's just aggravating back there running his mouth. Let's just get rid of him."

"Not yet." Cyrus stated with a smile. He released the grip from Cassandra's throat. She stepped away.

Malivick raised his head to Cyrus once again. "You just can't kill your brother." He said.

Cyrus spun around and landed a mighty punch across Malivick's face. The chains once again jerked tightly.

"Now, let's go." Cyrus said with authority. They moved out but Malivick could barely stand much less walk with his fresh stab wound which bled badly.

"Uh. Cyrus." Nephtali uttered. "I think we have a problem." The captors were having to drag Malivick for the most part. This could slow them down quite a bit.

Malivick limped over in pain. "I can't walk on this leg." He said. "I guess you'll have to kill me now." Cyrus turned and lowered his head in disgust.

The captor that held Malivick's left shoulder dropped him, and gave up. "I'm not carrying this guy with us." The captor said.

Cyrus pulled out his side arm and approached. "You will carry him if I tell you to carry him!" Cyrus said. The captor quickly rethought his strategy in silence.

"Come on Cyrus! Just kill me!" Malivick yelled. "Either way, you will not succeed!"

Cassandra couldn't listen to it anymore. "You want to die so bad." She said, "I'll take care of you." Cassandra pulled out her pistol and took aim at Malivick's head.

"Go ahead Cassandra." Malivick said methodically. "DO IT! Pull the trigger!" Malivick was silenced by two gunshots. Blood splattered on Malivick's face. He hesitantly looked down to see Cassandra shot dead.

"Now, what we're you saying?" Cyrus asked. He pointed the gun back in the captor's face.

Malivick ripped on his chains with all his strength. "Why did you kill her!? God damn you Cyrus!" Malivick yelled.

The frightened captor looked for support from the others. "Come on you idiots, help me." He demanded.

"On the contrary Malivick." Cyrus laughed. "It is our god who is damning you!" Cyrus' evil grin turned to complete seriousness. Cyrus landed another enormous punch to Malivick's temple. The severe blow knocked him unconscious.

Nephtali was somewhat stunned, but the group moved out as Cassandra's dead body was left behind.

They moved into a covered area just ahead of a small city.

While the group moved quietly, Malivick's head erupted with the voice of the Hooded Vampire. "Malivick. Time is running incredibly short. You have to stop Cyrus now." The disembodied voice rang out in Malivick's mind.

I can't feel my body. Malivick's breath was short, his life force drained.

I've done everything asked of me.

In the midst of Malivick's dreamlike conversation, Cyrus and the others began taking fire from humans hiding in the distance. At first it was just two shooters. The vampires took cover behind the corner of a wall and Nephtali waited for the fire to cease and then fired off a few blind shots with his M-16.

Deep inside Malivick's mind the familiar voice of the cloaked vampire rang loud and clear. "I've been very patient with you." The voice echoed. "But now is the time to act. You are the only thing standing in the way of death for every human. You can still defeat your brother. I know that you can do this." More soldiers arrived to help against the vampires. Cyrus and Nephtali were shooting at the soldier. Cyrus wielded two pistols in a desperate act. "Shit! There's more!" He shouted. "You three get over here and help!" Cyrus screamed. "Where the hell are our troops!?"

The three captors threw Malivick's lifeless body to the ground and moved in to support Cyrus and Nephtali against the human resistance.

Malivick's eyes opened and he pulled himself together. His expression displayed his effortless determination to escape. He stretched his arms and pulled tightly on his shackles. It only put him in more pain. His leg was bloody and the weakness showed. Nephtali took a shot right through the chest and went down.

Two of the captors dragged him to safety, as the third captor grabbed Malivick and pointed the gun at his temple.

Malivick snapped the chains on his shackles, grabbed the barrel of the vampires gun, and pointed it down. The captor inadvertently fired several rounds that hit the injured Nephtali and killed him immediately. Malivick disarmed the captor and dropped to his back. He put his legs up and shot through his leg shackles also fatally wounding the captor.

Just as Cyrus looked over, Malivick was firing two shots in the back of the second captor's head. He killed the beast instantly. But before he could get to his feet, Cyrus aimed one pistol at Malivick while he fired the second gun at the soldiers. The brothers made eye contact for only a moment. Cyrus fired three shots, all piercing his brothers chest. Malivick fell to the ground, lifeless in a pool of blood.

Cyrus and the final captor were taking too much fire and had to fall back. Cyrus went over to Malivick and checked his pulse and heartbeat. "Sorry, it had to end like this Malivick." Cyrus said.

"Come on Cyrus, let's get out of here." The final captor reloaded. He was ready to move out.

"No." Cyrus said with a hint of regret in his tone.

The vampire snarled in disgust. "What?" The captor torched.

"You stay here and fight." Cyrus said. "Until the death."

Cyrus ran off as the soldiers cleared the area and moved in closer. The vampire captor was ripped to pieces by the automatic gun fire from the human weapons.

Of all the bodies around, Cyrus' wasn't one of them.

CHAPTER TWENTYFOUR

"No Escape"

"The ultimate measure of a man is not where he stands
in moments of comfort, but when he stands at times of
challenges and controversy."
- Dr. Martin Luther King Jr.

Deep in the African Jungle, in the dead of night a fierce and intense battle was underway in dozens of small villages. The relentless attack continued as vampires tore through the humans throats with their teeth. Many humans tried to fight back, but soon the toxins kicked in and they fell into death sleep.

Moments later the victims began to regain consciousness as a reborn, and immediately fed on the nearest sensed human flesh. Living or dead.

United States Top Secret Underground Headquarters

The President of the United States watched on in horror of a video shot on a hand held video camera by a local businessman in Africa. He watched as the cameraman ran to escape the terror, only to trip over some debris and be decimated by the vicious vampires. "Where did you get this?" The President demanded.

"We're not sure, it was sent to us anonymously. We assume it is authentic." Lamar Guthry, the State Secretary said.

"I cannot believe these, creatures." The President sobbed.

Philip hovered over the main computer in a trance. "Mister President on the screen here are numbers from a scientific readout of human casualties domestically and worldwide." Walker said. "After the nuclear explosion and up until an hour ago the number deaths in the United States was over eight hundred million people. Over three and a half billion have been killed world wide." The President sat in silence and shook his head.

The Vice President entered and carried paper readouts. "Sir, infantry and armored units are in position." She said with a shimmer of hope.

The President raised his head and looked at the screen. "Tell them they are authorized to fire at the target." He gave his orders with haste, he was hoping there was enough time. He still wished there was another way.

"Yes sir." Linda replied. The large projection screen above them flickered along with the rest of the lights in the bunker. All the computer systems restarted.

"What the hell?" The President wondered aloud. Immediately two technicians entered the room.

"We have a problem!" One of them said.

The lights flickered then went off all together. A few moments later the back up generator kicked in.

Philip was able to exhale as the emergency lights came on.

"I'll say we have a problem." Philip said. "We just lost contact with the unit and our defenses."

"What? How?" The President asked.

One of the technicians responded, "Just a second ago I had red flags off the Pacific coast."

"More nukes!" Walker wailed.

"Three bases were activated." The technician tried to disable the launch sequence.

Linda re-entered the room with a scowl. "Satellite imagery has been interrupted." She said.

The President sat back down in the chair. "At this point. What could I possibly do?" He asked his remaining constituents.

"I guess this is a bad time to mention the nuclear warheads will be ready for launch in one hundred-twenty minutes." Lamar Guthry added factiously. "We have no way to disarm them without power."

"Of course not. Well, that's it then." The President sat back firmly in his final resting place.

CHAPTER TWENTYFIVE
"The Resurrection"

"A man that wants nothing is invincible."

D irectly above Malivick, the light of Julian burned brightly in the night sky. Once again the voice of the cloaked vampire echoed in Malivick's head. "What are you doing Malivick?" The voice began. "Get up! I told you what you have to do. Malivick, get up. Cyrus is almost at the temple. This is not your time to die. Not now. Kill Cyrus before he reads that enchantment."

It's too late. I can feel it.
"It's not too late." The voice echoed.
They have accomplished their goal. I have failed.
"You must go now. Wake up!" The enchanting voice said.

Suddenly Malivick was standing tall. He had no idea why he was still alive, but that didn't matter right now. Fires burned all around as he gathered his thoughts. Miraculously Malivick was healed, the gunshot and the stab wounds were closed. He looked around at the devastation and moved off in the night.

Berlin, Germany

Cyrus rode shotgun with a vampire known as Striker. Striker drove the customized Jeep with thorough experience over the rough and jagged terrain. They pulled inside the palace walls of Berlin. The light of Julian burned directly above the vampire crescent symbol. "Let me out here." Cyrus told him. Striker idled the Jeep to the near side entrance. Cyrus jumped out and hurried inside. "Get your gun and guard this door." Cyrus said. "Don't let anyone pass!"

"Got it." Striker replied. "We did it." Cyrus acknowledged the accomplishment.

Inside the ancient Eastern German temple, Cyrus walked down the middle of the Chapel Chambers with haste, just before dawn on the new year. Inside, Cyrus searched the walls for the enchantment.

Back outside, Malivick appeared on a motorcycle that seemed to have incurred minor body damage. He followed the Light of Julian to the temple as the sun began to break the horizon. He saw the Jeep and immediately took fire from Striker. Malivick ditched the bike and fired back.

Three more vampires showed up behind Malivick. He fought off two of them, but took a devastating kick from the third, which misfired a round from his gun. That round luckily enough was the one that hit Striker and put him out of action.

Malivick faced off against the three defenders. They were obviously reborn vampires less powerful and coherent than soldier vampires. Two more showed up and he suddenly had his hands full.

Malivick didn't hold back, despite the desperate odds. His intentions and will were so great it lifted his abilities above his opponents. Malivick was wielding his sword in one hand and an automatic rifle in the other. He was able to keep the vampires at bay, and picked them off one at a time. On top of the first five, three more appeared. A bullet from a vampire's gun ricocheted off Malivick's sword and missed him by mere centimeters. Finally with a few more strategic shots he put the other rabid vampires down. Malivick headed around the corner to get inside the temple and stop his brother. But Malivick ran into about ten German Soldiers just as they clicked back the hammer on their guns.

Malivick dropped his sword and gun.

"Freeze! You a vampire, yes?" A large German soldier asked.

"Friend." Malivick offered to drop his weapons.

There was a moment where Malivick thought he might be safe. "No. Kill him!" The soldier gave the order and immediately the others unloaded round after round at Malivick.

Incredibly Malivick waved his hands creating a forcefield that remarkably slowed the bullets before impact. He threw his arms forward and all the built up lead shot straight back at the stunned German soldiers. The rebel soldiers collapsed to the ground. Most were dead, and the rest were too injured to do anything. His powers had grown to amazing lengths.

CHAPTER TWENTYSIX

"The End ... of Everything"

"My brain is the key, that will set me free."
- Harry Houdini

Inside the underground German temple, Cyrus searched around in the pit area for some sort of key or lever. The temple was ancient and looked as if it had remained undisturbed for centuries. Among the ancient ruins and archaic structures in the room, Cyrus was amazed by a familiar looking coffin that sat inside the center of the room hidden by towering statues of prehistoric rulers and deities.

It was just like in his dreams. Cyrus brushed off the dust and looked for the inscription that he already knew was there.

This was it.

It was time to make history, so without hesitation Cyrus opened the coffin. The floor beneath his feet began to shake, his knees trembled. The ground separated just a meter away and raised up, exposing a stairway that led further underground.

Cyrus wasted no time and headed down the stairs and inside the tomb.

Malivick followed his brother in, not far behind, but someone even further back lurked in the shadows. Malivick navigated carefully and aimed his pistol into the stalking darkness.

Glass shattered nearby; Malivick moved around a corner and spotted Nike Wells who was coming right at him. "What's going on?" Malivick asked, surprised to see him. He was glad to see a friendly face.

"I got Cassandra's distress call. I got here as fast as I could." Nike looked worried.

"It's a good thing you came." Malivick told him. "Cassandra is working with Cyrus now. Or was anyway." He updated Nike on the situation, but he was stumped.

"What?" Nike asked, his chiseled stature was unusually slouched from the pain of war.

"No time to explain. Cyrus is inside." Malivick said. "We have to stop him." They moved further down in to the temple.

Avinalen Calender – New Years 2032
Modern Calender – December 21, 2012

Cyrus looked ahead in the underground area as the figure that was following him approached. He turned and aimed his gun point blank at the stalkers skull. "Roth!" Cyrus shouted. "You made it."

"I wouldn't miss it." Roth exclaimed.

Cyrus got back to the task at hand and continued to search for the prayer.

"The prayer should be engraved above his tomb." Cyrus said. "We are close, I can feel it." Roth and Cyrus moved a little further through the darkness and came to a dead end.

The wall was littered with ancient Aramaic engravings. Cyrus didn't think twice as to how such engravings could have made it to that part of the world. He approached the wall and mumbled something in the language of origin. Suddenly the ground beneath the two began to lower.

Malivick and Nike interrupted and jumped down onto the platform as it continued to descend. Roth and Malivick exchanged fire as Cyrus leaped off the platform. He landed on the lowest level twenty feet below. "He's going after the tomb!" Malivick yelled to Nike.

Nike dove off after Cyrus, while Roth and Malivick continued to shoot it out. They soon resorted to hand to hand combat, and rolled around as the platform nearly reached the bottom.

On the ground Nike shot his pistol at Cyrus, but Cyrus was behind hard cover and used the moment to think of his next move. Nike waited for him to poke his head up. He thought he saw Cyrus duck behind a wall and Nike bit. He moved in on the location, but from the opposite side Cyrus emerged, and put two bullets in Nike's head.

Cyrus took off toward the tomb.

Still on the platform, Malivick continued beating on Roth. He landed a stiff kick and sent him to the edge. Malivick rolled over and snagged his gun and charged Roth.

They both fired, Roth missed, Malivick tackled him off the platform and they both landed below about fifteen feet. Malivick sat up and saw both Roth and Nike shot and bleeding, neither of them were moving.

"Shit! Nike!" Malivick rushed to his fallen friends side, but he was already dead.

Cyrus stood just yards away from Malivick, he wiped at the dust on a large stone slab, then blew on the stone pad that revealed the initials "ESJ" before an even larger coffin. He brushed off the wall covered in webs and uncovered the prayer in front of the tomb.

Malivick could hear the Aramaic chant from his brother close by. The prayer bellowed through the temple. Immediately, the bright lights from outside broke through the room and revealed that it indeed was Elias' tomb. Original scriptures were etched into the golden walls. A solid gold statue of Elias Julian sat in the corner. Cyrus felt his work was finished. "Welcome home father!" He shouted out loud.

The ground began to tremble and the building shook wildly.

Malivick lunged at Cyrus and the two fought as if they knew it would be the last. No guns. Just fists and the rest that hand to hand had to offer.

Malivick looked stronger than ever and the lights burned brighter than it ever had before. He went right for the kill, even while parts of the building were breaking off all around them and plunging into the sky like a vacuum. Their world was falling apart around them, but there was still fight in both of the brothers. Malivick was able to pin Cyrus down, then he grabbed a small blade from his brother's hand and sliced Cyrus' leg open. It was a severe wound.

The lights interrupted both Malivick and Cyrus. Nothing could be seen besides blinding white light.

Moments later when vision was restored, the sky continued to beam with a concentrated white light. Then, a shimmering gold figure appeared high in the sky. It floated down ever so slowly from the sky and hovered just above the ground.

In front of the figure was Malivick and Cyrus who were both on their knees and tied up by some sort of electric forcefield. A digital hologram that was an enormous virtual representation stood thousands of feet tall. The figure shrank down a bit but still loomed large in the vast white space.

Cyrus could barely hold his head up. "Father!" He was elated to have accomplished his mission, still intoxicated by the poison his mind had endured.

The figures voice roared across the lands. "I am not who you think I am." The figure stated. "There never was any Elias Julian,

Cyrus. He was just a myth. Just like the rest of the earth's curators that *we* created." Neither Malivick nor Cyrus knew what was going on as they watched on in terror. "All of the God's your people worship are just a myth that started at the beginning of the project by *us*."

Cyrus seemed to be broken from the spell he had been under. He was severely groggy with nearly fatal injuries. "Who the hell is us?" He had just enough energy to ask. The brothers eyes no longer glowed and their strength was exhausted.

"I am one of six current Science Creators of your universe." The figure continued. "The original science creators released hundreds of different types of literary scriptures in numerous languages. It was all propaganda. It was just an experiment to see if the belief of an ethical system would catch on. "

The entire atmosphere turned to red, as the human image transformed into a demonic beastly figure. "The readers became followers of a cult religion." The figure rumbled. "Some groups grew so large it became stronger than a cult. It became a lifestyle of belief in a God and more importantly, an ethics system. One group surpassed our expectations. The vampires. They not only grasped and embraced their beliefs, they evolved and transformed into something greater than we had created."

Neither Malivick or Cyrus had the energy or effort to look at the figure in the face as they continued to listen. "Through careful consideration from past hypothesis, we concluded that we must make a decision." The figure continued. "Get rid of the vampires and let humans continue the rule of Earth for eternity, when after only a few thousand years they had already betrayed their beliefs by their actions and thoughts." The Science Creator unleashed the truths of the worlds creations. "Or, we could take the elite vampires that remained pure while under perjury from the humans and start over with a new race on this planet. They believed and faithfully lived underground waiting for the return of a messiah that didn't exist."

"We were coming up on the mark-over period and the decision was difficult. We were quite fond of our human creation. We decided to adopt one of the main philosophies that the vampires created. Survival of the fittest, or natural selection. We could not destroy everything ourselves. So we put the humans in the biggest endurance challenge of all." The brothers heard and listened closely, but slowly thoughts from throughout life hit them all at once.

"The vampires succeeded in their task and remained pure." The creator continued, but for the moment the brothers were lost in their own mind. "So they have been chosen to rule the existence of earth forever. They get their Elias Julian." Malivick spoke up after barely moving his head.

"What about if humans would have won. Would their God return to govern over them?" Malivick asked.

"That, wouldn't happen." The creator vowed. "We chose vampires in the beginning."

Cyrus couldn't believe it. "Then why the war?! Millions of innocent people died." He was disgusted.

"We could not interfere with the process. After the last project failed we installed a parameter known as a mark-over. If the balance was interrupted and became uneven in any way, the universe would reset itself twelve thousand years." The glowing figure said. "We could however manipulate the variables causing a favorable outcome."

Cyrus grunted, obviously unsatisfied with this answer. "We created you both for the exact purpose you have served. We created you exactly equal to keep the balance throughout the war, and these final days." The figure bellowed forth.

"Why would you want an evil population ruling the earth?" Malivick asked suspiciously.

"Vampires are only evil in comparison to humans." The figure answered. "That is why we could not allow them to coexist together on this planet. Vampires were the prime choice to lead the next project." The science creator morphed into the Hooded Vampire that guided Malivick along his journey before the war. "You see. We influenced you both accordingly. Everything kept in complete harmony. An exact balance. It was perfect. Your loyalty and the pursuit of hope are some of the qualities that we built." These final words burned a hole through the brothers.

Cyrus fought to speak. "That you built?" He asked disgustedly. "You don't tell people how to act. That's not life. That is artificial intelligence."

"I didn't just make you say that, did I? Free will." The creator stated. "You have all that. We just chose you to lead an important role in life."

"I don't believe you." Cyrus said.

"This all had to happen this way. It had to." The figure went out of focus momentarily. "Our goal was to have a race identical to our image. The humans had it and lost it. The vampires changed our mind's of what our image is. With the new mark-over procedures in place we had to be precise. The last project failed, but our method was too catastrophic and damaged the planet severely."

"Will we have a roll in the new world?" Cyrus mustered the energy to ask.

"I'm afraid not." The creator explained. "After the killings cease there will be a four hundred year hiatus period, where nothing on this planet will exist. We will then spawn and start all over. I thought it was fair to reveal the truth to you. For all your hard work. You two are the only living beings to know how these things work."

A parting gift thats useless.

"What does it matter?" Malivick asked.

"After vampires kill all humans, they will turn on one another killing off the population." The creator said. "The one remaining will be reborn Elias Julian. That is the being that will be reincarnated and will take over creation of Earth." The figure paused. "I came to tell you that there is good news for you in all of this. There will be an afterlife, and that's when the real fun starts."

Malivick was near death from blood loss, but continued to fight to ask. "You created an afterlife?"

"Actually, no." The voice said. "It is a rare phenomenon we haven't been able to explain. But we do know it exists. We are just creators of this one universe. There are others just like this in other solar systems with creators just like us." The creator explained.

Cyrus mustered one last question that resonated with the creator, his brother, and himself. "And how did the creators get their powers to create? Who gave it to them?"

The figure began to get unfocused, and glowed heavily, then receded back into the sky. "To be quite honest." The figure echoed. "We don't really know." Red clouds filled the sky as blood poured down. "For our chosen, eventuality has arrived for you all."

All of the remaining human population along with the vampires around the world looked up to the sky on their dooms day as nuclear halo's erupted in the atmosphere from all points of the globe.

The systematic extermination of all life forms continued as the war waged on without the brothers at the helm.

– The End. For Now...

Find out what happens NEXT, in

Father of Darkness:
The Next Project Volume 2
February 2008

Also coming in 2008

Father of Darkness*: Followers of Julian*

For a more in depth look inside the world of

THE NEXT PROJECT,

log onto www.atomicalien.s5.com/fod to get in depth historic

articles, photos, and much more.

A Short Story

TAKE DOWN

Written by

Ryan C. Stith

1.

Bruce Carmen picks up his office phone and presses speed dial one. The number dials up Special Agent Arthur Santiago's cell phone. Santiago has been the lead undercover agent on the Parello family investigation for more than two years, and he has gathered nearly enough evidence on the leaders of the operation to put the entire Las Vegas crime family behind bars for a very long time. Now he just has to escape the sting operation with his life.

The ringing stops and for a moment there is only silence, then a whisper. "Hold on." Arthur requests of his boss. Bruce's rugged figure asserts himself among the elite with his slick, outgoing, and charismatic behavior. Bruce just smirks as he listens to Santiago fumble around to get in safe talking distance. "Alright, what's up?" He now spoke casually without worry of being caught.

"Good news. The DA says we have enough to take in Vinny and his brother." Bruce says. Good news? For good news, Arthur doesn't sound very enthused, and with good reason.

TAKE DOWN

"Bruce, you know that's not going to work. We have to take them all at once or we could lose everything we've been working on for the last three years." Arthur is interrupted by his superior.

"Listen," Bruce pauses and gives a deep sigh. "That's why I'm calling you." He waits to see what Arthur will say, but there is only silence. "We need you to stay in a few more days."

Santiago finally broke his silence. "You have got to be kidding me." He knew Bruce wasn't kidding. "I have to get out now. I know Vinny is getting suspicious. My cover may have already been blown after the last job. I told you Bruce. You have to get me out!"

Bruce hates to hear his good friend so upset, especially when there is nothing that he can do about it. The orders come straight from the Federal Bureau of Investigation's Intelligence Director. "I'm sorry Arthur." Carmen does his best to assure Arthur it will be over soon. "Doug said that all intelligence points to this next job as the one that will go down in history. He wants you to stay on the inside until the bust when we take down everyone. Then you'll be safe to come out. We will have three tactical teams on standby, there is no danger Art."

More silence followed by a slew of curse words. "I have to go. Someone's here. Bruce get me out of here now! They know someone is working on the inside. Twenty four hours and I'm taking myself out." Bruce doesn't like being threatened.

"Listen Arthur I said...Hello?" Santiago already hung up. "Damnit!" Bruce slams his phone down. He sits back a moment then adjusts his tie and parts his hair. He stands up, grabs his coat, and exits out his office door.

2.

  Just outside the Las Vegas city limits north of the strip, Vincent "Vinny" Parello is pulling into a home owned by his younger brother Joseph Parello and has been the family home for three generations. Vincent's driver put the Cadillac in park and quickly made his way to the passengers door to let Vinny out as family captains stood by awaiting his arrival.

  "Pull the car around back. I'll call you when I'm ready." Vincent tells his driver. He grabs his cell phone and a brown paper bag, "Eddie!" The others join him on the walkway in front of the house.

  "Good to see you again Vinny." Eddie Dover was a legit businessman that helped the Parello family business keep a somewhat clean image for the past fifteen years or so.

  Vincent hugs the other gentleman and follows them into the house. "I hope you don't mind, I brought a bottle along to celebrate. I know you stopped drinking and all." Vinny pulls the bottle of whiskey from the paper bag in his hand.

"Are you kidding?" Eddie shouts. "I was just saying that to shut my wife up. Give me that!" He grabs the bottle from Vincent and follows the others inside.

Later on at the dinner table Vincent, Eddie, and two other Parello bosses, Walter Parello and Lonnie Patrick Parello were finishing up the fine steak dinner. The Johnny Walker Red Label bottle was empty and the men were just getting down to business.

Walter comes to the table and hands a folder to each of the others. "Here are the figures from what we made off the cars." Vincent opens the folder and looks over each of the classic hot rod cars that were stolen from an auction port and sold on the black market.

"Boy that Camaro was so sweet. I could have had some fun with that one." Vinny looks over at the others. A dark brown fedora covers Vincent's receding hairline. He pushes his black framed glasses up over his nose and focuses on the papers in front of him.

Eddie laughs as he flips through the pages. "It went for two hundred fifty thousand, not bad. I didn't expect it to top one fifty."

"Your crazy! Camaro's are the staple of American muscle." Lonnie has a strong opinion on the matter. He shut the folder and stands up from the dinner table. "So what is this big job you wanted to talk about Vincent?" Lonnie stretched off the buzz and leaned up against the wall next to Vinny.

Vincent lays the folder down and pulls a folded up piece of paper from his shirt pocket. He unfolds it and hands it to Eddie. "Ed, I've always trusted your opinion. What do you think about this take?"

"Where did you get this?" Eddie gazes at the pictures of three paintings.

"A friend. They are going on auction in about an hour, and I plan to take them." The others erupt in laughter thinking surely he must be kidding. But Vinny isn't laughing.

"These were the paintings taken from your father." Eddie knew the history of the Parello's very well. "How? I mean. One hour is not much time."

Vincent interrupts. "It's already in place. I have a team ready and waiting." He sits back in his chair. "One hour is plenty of time."

"I don't know if its the best time right now Vinny. The feds are all over our ass after last week. Luckily we got rid of the cars as fast as we did." Eddie doesn't like the idea.

"There is a reason they were on our ass after that last job, and that reason has been taken care of." Vincent didn't elaborate, but the others had a feeling that they knew what he was talking about.

Finally after the brief silence Walter asks, "So who is doing the job? Joe?" Vinny smiles.

"I have a team." Vinny pauses. "Well it's the same team that helped us with the cars. Christopher and the crew are already in place." He stands up from the table. "Joesph and Gabriel are going to work as decoy's to setup the heist. By the time it's all over, we'll have the paintings, the money, the rat will be taken down, and we all will be in the clear. I'll explain the details in a bit, but first. Dessert!" Vincent heads off into the kitchen. He comes back moments later with a box of cigars. The boys follow Vinny out to smoking room for more drinks and discussion.

3.

Downtown at the Police Department inside holding room C is Christopher Holt. He sits alone inside the dimly lit room fitted with a large glass two way mirror adjacent of the only exit. The door opens and Detective Ron Bass enters. He flips the light switch and the room lit up. Christopher Holt just stares at the detective as another officer enters and stands by as Detective Bass sits down across from Chris Holt. Bass is a large man with a short fuse and no tolerance for incompetence. He remained quiet and lights up a cigarette, as he blows the smoke right into Chris's face. "Listen Chris. We're going to give you one more chance to come clean."

"Smoking is bad for you." Chris's response doesn't faze Detective Bass. He just cocks a grin and slides in closer to Chris's face.

Once again Bass exhales a huge plume of smoke in Chris's face. "We already know that your lying. I know your not retarded. So STOP ACTING!"

TAKE DOWN

Chris shakes his head. "Not retarded. Mentally disabled, sir." He doesn't seem threatened by the taunting officer.

"I don't believe you. And your going to jail for a long time, unless you tell me what part you played in the heist of those cars!" Ron slams his hand down on the table and Chris jumps back in his seat.

"I don't know how to drive. I don't even have a license." Chris tries to explain he has nothing to do with it. "I've never stolen anything." Detective Bass grabs him by the arm.

Chris attempts to pull away but Bass is much much stronger and easily holds him still. He becomes easily frightened as the detective holds the lit cigarette over Chris's hand. "Tell me who hired you to steal those cars!" Ron shouts as he presses the burning tip of the cigarette into the top of his hand.

Chris screams in pain. "Help! I didn't do anything! I Swear! Please stop!" Detective Bass releases his grip on Chris. Chris pulls away and cradles his hand.

"Alright. Alright... You want to go to jail? Fine." Detective Bass seems to be through trying to get any information from Chris, when suddenly he lunges across the table and grabs Chris by the throat. "You know you won't make it one day inside! You better give it up now if you want any kind of deal!" Ron Bass grips his hands even tighter around Chris's neck as Chris's face turns blue. The screaming stops as he is barely able to let out a gasp. The other officer in the room even starts to worry as he steps forward about to interrupt when the door flies open and two men enter in a hurry.

TAKE DOWN

Detective Bass releases the stranglehold and Chris collapses out of his chair and to the ground. Ron Bass stands up face to face with the men. "Who the hell are you?"

The taller of the two steps forward. "I'm Agent Clancy and this is Agent Wilson, we're from the Federal Bureau of Investigation. What's going on here?" Agent Clancy looks at Chris's bright red face as he gasps for air on the floor.

"I was just about to get a confession before you busted in!" Ron Bass is certain of this.

"Is that so? Or were you just about to force him to tell you whatever you want to hear?" The second man, Agent Wilson kneels over Chris and helps him back into the chair. "Now Officer Bass. Wait outside. I want to have a word with you when I am finished in here." Agent Clancy stares into Bass's eyes waiting for him to leave.

"It's Detective Bass." Ron mutters.

"I said wait outside!" Agent Clancy makes his orders clear. Ron Bass and the other officer exits the room and the door shuts behind them. Clancy sits down across from Chris and pours him a glass of water.

"Thank you." Chris replies as he takes a drink from the Styrofoam cup. "Bad man burned me." He holds his hand up and shows the burn mark from the cigarette.

"We'll get someone to take a look at it. Don't worry Chris your safe." FBI Agent Clancy leans in to say something to Chris when his phone rings. He sits back and looks at the number calling. "Listen Chris I really don't think you had anything to do with that robbery. I'm going to have one of the officers take you home okay? I have to take this phone call. But just hold on and someone will come in and look at that hand." Clancy answers the phone as he exits the holding room. As the door closes behind him, he covers his cell phone to speak with Detective Bass. "I want you to get an officer to process Mister Holt's paperwork and release him immediately." Agent Clancy starts off down the hall, but Ron Bass stops him.

"What the hell do you mean release him? That kid had something to do with that heist!" Detective Bass follows Clancy through the lobby.

Agent Clancy hangs up his phone to concentrate on Bass. "He's not going to give in holding him here. Don't worry about it anyway, its not your case anymore. It's now a federal matter and the last thing you will have to do for this case is finish Holt's release papers. Now do it." Clancy turns around and walks away before Ron could say another word.

Minutes later at the discharge desk Chris Holt is being unhand-cuffed and is given his paperwork. The officer offers to give Chris a ride home, but he wants to ride the bus and he heads out the front door to the nearby bus stop.

Chris walks past the street corner and hurries down a side ally. His cell phone rings and he pulls it from his pocket. "Hey, Vinny." He pauses as Chris looks around to make sure he isn't being followed. "Listen, I can't talk right now. I just got picked up by the fuzz, and they questioned me about the cars. I'll call you when I can talk safely." Chris walks faster crossing a few more blocks and stops at a pay phone. He plunks in some change and dials back up to Vincent Parello.

TAKE DOWN

"Alright, it's me." Chris looks at his watch. It's half past six o'clock. "No I didn't tell them anything, but I don't think they bought the handicap story. They didn't mention your name so I wouldn't worry." He looks around, paranoid someone is watching. "I know they are waiting on me. I am on my way. No don't call the job off, we'll be fine. They don't have a clue, I'm telling you." Chris does his best to cover his face as cars goes by. "Already on my way. I'll call you when I'm in position." Chris hangs up the pay phone and jogs off down the street.

4.

Minute after minute passes as Joseph Parello and Gabriel Dozell sit in the Conference Room of the Echo Casino Plaza waiting for their signal. Vincent Parello's brother Joseph whose nickname is Slasher for devious reasons, glances at his watch getting anxious as the time frame quickly nears expiration.

Across the room two security guards stand by watching for any suspicious activities.

The auction items were being transported from a secure vault to the facility via armored truck under heavy police support. The items were displayed in the conference room for all to see and after the item was sold it was once again transported back to the secure facility until the purchaser deposits payment of the entire price for the acquisition. The Vercelli Paintings which are the target of the job are about to leave the facility in less than twenty minutes, which means unless Chris gets in position soon the job may be called off.

5.

On the opposite side of the casino compound, north of the Conference Center is the secured building that houses the main vaults. Inside are a half dozen armed guards scattered throughout the building. Security has been stepped up while auction items are being held here.

Out back of the facility Jules Fiengold, who works as a janitor in the casino offices is dumping garbage cans in the dumpster. He finishes the last can and puts the container back on the four wheel cart and heads back inside under security supervision. He removes his access card from his shirt pocket and slides it through the scanner. The light turns green and a loud buzzing unlocks the door. Jules pulls the door outward, wheels the cart inside making sure the door shuts behind him.

Back inside he pulls the four trash bins off the cart and stacks them carefully. He drags them behind him through the metal detector leading past the security checkpoint, but the censor goes off alerting the guards of something Jules is carrying.

TAKE DOWN

Jules looks all about him for the source. "Ahh. This new tool belt. I haven't quite gotten used to having it on me at all times. Sorry about that Mark." He tells the guard stationed at the metal detector. "All this metal on it you'd think I'd learn by now." Jules removes his tool belt and sets in on the side and walks through again. This time nothing. It was the tool belt. Thank god.

"No worries Fiengold. Have a good one." The security guard sees his way through the checkpoint and back into the facility.

Jules pushes his cart with his tool belt on top down the hallway, and when the hall hits a dead end he takes a right. Jules opens the door to a maintenance room that is more less the size of a broom closet. He pushes the cart halfway inside and pulls the lid off of the first trash bin. Chris Holt pops out gasping for air while still trying to stay quiet.

"What took you so long?" Chris whispers as Jules looks around to make sure no one is around. Jules knows there is security all around the perimeter tonight.

"Quit whining and get out of there. Do you have the guns?" Jules looks inside the bin for his pistol. Inside a black cloth wrap, three pistols, and a fairly large toolkit that Chris grabs right away. He then takes two pistols and loads the clips, then holsters his weapons. "Okay Chris, it's all on you now." Jules pats him on the back in some sort of comforting effort. But Chris is ready.

"You know you scared the daylights out of me when that alarm went off." Chris tells Jules half joking. He moves off down the hall way and peaks around corner to elude detection. Jules just laughs to himself quietly as he puts the chrome clip into his 9mm handgun.

TAKE DOWN

The layout of this part of the casino is like a maze and it's that way for a reason. If anyone that wasn't supposed to be there got in, they would be discovered instantly by easily getting lost. It's a good thing Chris is a professional at this sort of thing. He comes to a corner and pulls back just as two guards walk by him. Chris stood completely still as the two security guards kept on walking without noticing a thing. He swallows the lump in his throat and keeps moving.

6.

Just a few blocks from the casino, a white closed paneled work truck circled Grand Avenue down to Third street and around the four blocks repeatedly. The driver, Marse Virgil works for Vincent Parello and as he circles by the casino he continues to notice suspicious behavior that could be the police about to move in. Marse is supposed to wait for word from the boss, but it's been a while and he hasn't heard anything.

Mob captain Marse Virgil decides to park the truck and get involved. He finds a good spot for the van and then hops out and heads in. But just a few seconds later his cell rings. It's Vincent. Finally.

7.

One of the suspicious trucks Marse noticed is parked just one block south of the casino, on the side of the street. It was an oversize box truck that just seemed out of place.

Inside was actually a mobile command center for the Las Vegas Police Department Vice unit. Three detectives were camped out inside the truck viewing numerous hidden camera feeds and tapping in on multiple conversations.

The lieutenant in charge of the surveillance team is Detective Ron Bass. He sits quietly observing the action on the monitor, constantly clicking the mouse to alternate camera views. Two other technicians sit back to back with Bass facing two other monitors with four screens on each. They all have independent audio output and were listening for any signals about a hit by the mob.

Ron Bass is watching live footage from inside the auction lobby. More specifically, Joseph Parello and Gabriel Dozell are center frame on the surveillance camera from inside. "Come on Joe, make a move..." Ron is anxious as he waits for any sign of unusual behavior.

Back inside the Casino Conference center where Joe and Gabriel sit observing the auction from nearly the back row, things are going off without a hitch. Although the mob pair have no idea if the job is still on. Making any outside communication would give them up easily. Suddenly an ear piercing alarm rings out inside the Casino Conference center.

"Well here we go." Gabriel leans in and tells Joseph so that only he can hear. The two look around just like all the others in the room. No one seems to know what was going on. A few people panic and head for the door.

FBI Director Bruce Carmen is listening in on chatter from inside the auction area, once the alarm sounds Bruce looks to the monitors covering outside the casino. He notices a police set-up and knows the police are about to move in. "Shit! Get on the phone with PD and find out who is running the raid on the casino! Find out and tell them to hold! Do not let them move in!" Bruce shouts to his assistant. "Call, now!"

On the street side in the LVPD Vice truck Ron Bass gets word of the alarm and must make a decision. Units are moving into position, but Bass has to give the word. He sits there and continues watching the casino lobby on the monitor. But strangely nothing looked out of place. Joseph and Gabriel haven't moved from their seats. "Something isn't right." Bass says to himself.

The officer standing behind Ron speaks up. "Sir, we need your authorization, now." The officer is on the phone with the unit waiting right outside the casino conference center doors.

TAKE DOWN

"Alright, move in. Take the two Parello boys and watch out for anyone else on that list." Ron gives in to the moment, and the word is sent to the vice unit to move in.

Inside, the auction is being evacuated. The dozens of auction goers flood through the emergency exits and out the building. The police capture Gabriel Dozell first as he is near the exit; they take him down without incident. Joseph Parello doesn't go quite as easy.

Someone grabs Joseph by the shoulder. "Hey, get your hands off of me. Hey! What the hell?!" Joseph plays along as if he has no idea what is happening. Three swat members jump Joseph, throw him to the ground to get him in cuffs, then lead him out the front door and into police custody.

8.

"Damnit!" Bruce Carmen shouts as he slams the phone down. "They moved in on Parello. Son of a bitch! They're going to screw it all up, if they send a unit into the vault." Bruce's assistant just sits there listening to his boss, when suddenly Bruce jumps up from his seat and leaves the room in a hurry.

Christopher Holt looks up at the vault door as if it was his grand challenge. The door to the hallway closes behind him. He is almost home free. Chris pulls out the set of tools he brought along with him. He unravels the kit and just as he is about to get started, he hears someone behind him entering in the code on the door. "Fantastic!" Chris rolls his eyes, slightly panicked. He wraps up the kit while looking for a place to hide in the brightly lit, open ended room. He can hear voices outside the door.

"For some reason the key code isn't working." A voice outside the door sounded muffled. Five swat members and two casino officials are standing just outside in the hallway, as an official radio transmission crackled across the officers walkies.

TAKE DOWN

"Zero Wolf, pull back. Your orders are to pull back! The FBI is taking over the investigation and we have direct orders not to breach the vault." The orders are given, but there is hesitation. "Zero Wolf, do you copy?"

"Zero Wolf, copy. We've already entered. Pulling back now." The voice outside sounded like Ron Bass. "Listen, those FBI pricks are getting on my nerves. Swat unit take Mr. Bonilla and get back to station. I'm checking the vault." Bass sounds determined to do things his way.

"But sir. Our orders were ..." A different voice, this time, one of the swat officers spoke up.

Detective Ron Bass doesn't want to hear it. "I gave you your order. Now go!" The police unit files off and leaves the casino manager and Detective Ron Bass alone, still trying to get the key code to work. "Step aside."

Bass moves the casino manager from the door way and with one stiff kick, busts the door in, nearly off the hinges. Inside is clear, there is no sign of Chris anywhere. After Bass clears the room the casino manager enters and heads for the vault doors. "Go ahead. Open it." The detective tells him.

The manager first enters the unique sixteen digit key code, followed by fingerprint verification. The final step is voice confirmation, and just as the casino manager spoke the code word; the vault door made a loud clank followed by a thunderous rumble from inside the vault.

Chris Holt appears behind Ron Bass who watches as the vault door opens. He's hanging upside down from inside the ceiling. He flips down onto his feet alerting Ron Bass. Bass turns around to fire, but Chris is too fast as he grabs onto the detective's gun. Chris rips the gun right from his, then throws him to the ground inside the vault.

TAKE DOWN

"Get on the ground!" Chris yells at the casino manager, who now is scared mindless. "Listen! I am FBI Agent Arthur Santiago." He told the two, while aiming the gun point blank at Bass. "I am working undercover to expose the Parello crime family. You are interfering with a federal investigation."

"Ahh shit. I'm sorry about earlier man. I had no idea." Ron Bass now had to worry about losing his job. He didn't know what else to say.

Holt, now identified as Arthur Santiago moves inside the vault. "Quiet! Don't move! Do you understand?" Santiago looks around the room, while keeping an eye on the two. He sees the paintings and goes straight for them. He knows time is short, and transfers the art work to a cylinder cannister. "Give me your gear." Arthur tells Ron Bass. He takes Ron's kevlar vest, helmet, and gun.

"It will be safer for you two to stay here until I come back. Just sit tight." Arthur doesn't waste any time and hops out of the vault with the artwork in tote. He closes the vault door behind him sealing the only ones aware of his presence, inside.

Arthur opens the door leading to the hallway just enough to peak out. He makes sure the coast is clear, then tracks off down the narrow corridor. Arthur approaches a dead end with a pair of doors labeled, 'Maintenance'. He tries the handle, but the door is locked. He pulls a lock pick from the swat vest and pops the lock and goes inside.

He moves to the corner of the room where a chute like device runs from the top level all the way down. It's used for easy transport of garbage. Arthur ensures that all three paintings are secured in one of the tubes and drops it down the chute. He looks down to see it fall, but the darkness quickly takes it out of sight.

Arthur pulls his cell phone from his pocket and heads back out and down the hallway. "Jules, it's Chris. Part one is complete. Move on to the next step." He reaches back where he came in and pulls the pair of goggles on his head to shield his face from being noticed. Arthur hangs up the cell phone and turns the power off.

Jules Feingold's shift is ending just in time. He hurries into the restroom carrying a large duffel bag. Just moments later he emerges from the stall dressed in full police uniform. He heads off silently, navigating to the entrance of the storage facility.

He comes to a stop just before exiting the building when he sees the group of six officers. He pauses only a minute to take a deep breath, and then approaches the swat crew.

"Gentlemen! I just got off the phone with Detective Bass." Jules tells the commanding officer. "He told me to tell you that the vault is clear and to get back to the auction house immediately." He's hoping they will buy it.

"What? Well, where is he?" The swat leader asks the unusual character. "Do I know you?" He continues to prod Jules with questions.

Jules was sweating under his helmet and goggles. "Don't question my authority Greene! Bass is still going through the inventory with the casino manager." Quick thinking helps put Jules back on the same page with the other officers. "Now get back to the auction house, there is a 413!" That gets the officers moving. They load up in the swat truck and within seconds they are gone. It seems Arthur, or Christopher is in the clear.

9.

Back at the illustrious Parello home, Vincent Parello dials Chris Holt's cell phone number for the fifth time without an answer. Vinny isn't a very trusting guy. You can't be in this business, because at any time your very best friend could stab you in the back. "Son of a bitch!" Vinny hangs up the phone. "I know he's playing us. If I get my hands on him.." He takes a deep breath, trying to calm his anger.

He thinks for a few seconds, then picks up the phone and dials a different number. "Hey. Marse, listen Chris turned his phone off, and I want to know what the hell is going on. Get everyone together and get inside there. Call me back when you find him." Vincent is just about to hang up, but listens and Marse continues to talk. "No, I don't care if the cops are inside, you get in there and find those paintings!" Vincent slams down the phone and sits back in the chair at his desk. He takes a sip from the glass in his hand. Whiskey straight up for the veteran drinker. Vincent grips his head and massages his temple. He opens the top drawer of the desk and takes out two aspirin. He drops them onto his tongue and downs the rest of the whiskey.

TAKE DOWN

Marse Virgil, gun in hand moves to the exterior wall of the storage facility. "Marse! Over here." Jules Feingold appears from around the corner waving Marse inside the entrance that he has just dispatched the swat team from.

"Hey Jules. Have you heard from Chris?" Marse looks around as they entered the facility. Oddly enough, there isn't anyone around to stop their progress.

"I talked to him just a few minutes ago. He said that he had the paintings with him." Jules tells him.

Marse seems to think somethings up. "Vinny told me that Chris turned his phone off and wasn't answering him. The boss got worried and wants us to find Chris." He replies scratching his head. Marse's shaved blond hair accentuated the blood rushing to his face.

Jules looks around for the police. He is always paranoid like that. "Everything was going according to plan the last I hea.... Is that?" Jules squints and covers the sunlight from his eyes. "It is them! Lonnie and Walter are coming this way." Jules leads Marse inside as the other two Parello's join up with them in the lobby.

Now back at the mobile police headquarters, both swat units are meeting up and now realize Detective Bass didn't give any orders. And now he's missing. Inside the vice surveillance truck the swat members get a message from command. One of the two police technicians emerges from the truck to relay the message to the officers.

TAKE DOWN

"Sargent Greene. We still haven't heard back from detective Bass, and we just got word that Walter and Lonnie Patrick Parello are on the premises." The technician tells the observing warriors.

Greene knew they had been tricked. "Where?" He asks even though he already knew.

"Back at the storage vault." The tech didn't even finish getting his words out, before the Sargent had readied his weapon. "Greene! It's still the Fed's gig!" He shouts to the officers who are following Greene to the truck.

"Screw them!" Greene shouts back as the swat unit peels off down the street in the modified hummer pickup, back toward the vault.

Inside the lobby of the storage facility Jules, Marse, Walter, and Lonnie all stand huddled by the security entrance as Jules fumbled with the surveillance equipment. "There. It's disabled." Jules says as he separates wiring from the power box. He continues back inside and holds the door for the others. "We need to go straight back and then to the right. Chris has to be in here somewhere. And don't worry, the building was evacuated already." That is reassuring, but the hardened criminals keep their handguns ready anyway. They casually move down the hallway, watching one another's back.

Jules reaches the corner first and then moves a little quicker, after taking a right at the end of the hall. "Maybe we should split up." Lonnie whispers to Jules.

"Nah. I'm the only one that knows my way around this building. Trust me it's like a maze. Somethings not right. I just talked to Chris a few minutes ago." Jules tells the others, who are wondering which way to go next.

TAKE DOWN

"FREEZE! Las Vegas Police! Put your guns on the ground now!!" Swat Sargent Greene yells at the Parello boys. Lonnie and Walter froze alright. But they were just waiting for a chance to make their move. Marse and Jules aren't as experienced in having guns pointed at their faces, and wasn't sure what to do. "I said put your guns on the ground, NOW!!" Greene repeats his orders.

"Alright, alright." Marse breaks the silence, and started to place his pistol on the ground. He looks at Walter who gives him a slight wink and follows Marse in putting down his weapon.

Lonnie plays along. "What the hell Walter? Don't do it! Get your gun!" He shouts at Walter Parello, trying to get the group out alive.

"SHUT UP!" The swat crew becomes uneasy with the situation and wants to move in on the gang. "DROP IT!" The mind games continue.

"I'm putting it down. Don't shoot!" Walter responds as he places his pistol on the ground. He slowly pulls his hand away.

"Now get on the ground. You two, drop your gun NOW." Sargent Greene screams at the mobsters. "Last chance!"

Walter stands back to his feet, ducks low and reveals a sub machine gun under his coat. Without hesitation Walter fires at the SWAT team, launching everyone into a lethally intense gun battle. The officers waste no time and return automatic suppression fire as the four mobsters evade behind the corner of the wall.

Lonnie pulls out his matching SMG automatic weapon, and fires blindly from around the corner. He puts one SWAT officer down with a lucky shot. Just seconds later Marse stretches for his gun that lays just beyond his reach. He stretches a bit to far and takes two rounds through the shoulder. Marse collapses to the ground, groaning and clutching his chest.

Jules grabs Marse by the leg and pulls him back from the line of fire. Blood smears along the floor as it continues to pour from Marse's chest. Walter puts two more cops down with strategically placed gunfire. SWAT began pulling back to help their injured, but as they retreat, the mobsters advance toward them. The gunfire continues and all men go spend clip after clip. Walter and Lonnie, veteran soldiers of the U.S. Army rush the remaining three SWAT officers and shoot it out, taking a few hits, but ultimately eliminating the offensive.

10.

Bruce Carmen can hear the gunfire inside the casino compound, from the surveillance recordings. "What the hell is going on inside there?" Carmen shouts, looking at his assistant. Bruce's office is transparent from nearly every angle. The appearance is a basic and modern one with a touch of elegance in sculptures and other artwork. Monitoring equipment is fully integrated into this office.

"Las Vegas Police moved in on the Parello's inside the vault compound. Multiple injuries." The assistant relays the real time information to his boss, who sits in front of the monitors, livid.

"Arthur is still inside there! We have to move now! Get Delta team on the line, tell them to move in. This is it!" Bruce Carmen jumps up, grabs his coat, and leaves his office for the scene.

11.

"Holy shit! We have to get out of here!" Jules shouts at Walter and Lonnie as he rushes back to Marse's side. "He's not breathing! We need to get him to a hospital, now!"

Walter pulls of his coat and ties it around the gunshot wound on his left arm. He approaches Jules, and takes Marse's pulse. "He's dead. We have to go now, or we'll be dead too. Let's find Chris and get the hell out of here!" Lonnie hears a door close behind him and instinctively turns to fire.

"Whoa! Don't shoot. It's me!" Christopher appears from around the corner. "I heard the shooting, What the ..." Chris sees the dead cops, and almost loses control.

"Are those the paintings?" Walter asks Chris, pointing at the cannister around his shoulder.

Chris is in shock from seeing six dead officers that he couldn't save. "Uhh.. uh, yeah. I have them."

"Good. Now let's get the hell out of here." Walter tells him. "Jules. Where is the back exit to this place? We can't walk out the front door. They know we're here."

Jules has to think for a second. "This way." He doesn't want to leave Marse behind, even though he knows its too late. He's already dead. The group moves along after Jules, Chris catches up to the front.

"Hey Jules, can you call Vinny and let him know everything is good?" Chris asks him, as they approach the deserted security checkpoint. "I'm sure he is wondering what's going on. My cell doesn't get any service in here."

Jules pulls his phone from the police vest he is wearing, and dials Vinny up. At that very second, two armed FBI agents enter through the rear exit, and approach the unaware mobsters.

"FBI! Freeze!" One of the agents yells, Jules looks up. But before he or any other mobster could make a move, Chris aims and fires four consecutive rounds. Both FBI agents collapse to the ground.

Walter looks at the two agents on the floor not moving. "Good work Chris. Now, let's go!" The four men pass through the security checkpoint and just a few steps closer to freedom.

12.

Just outside the Echo Casino secure storage compound, the Federal Bureau of Investigation is prepped and ready for the take down of the Parello empire. Three dozen law enforcement officials from the local and federal level are standing just meters away from the front door that Arthur is about to lead the mobsters through.

Miles away at the Parello home as well as several other key targets, numerous teams of federal agents were moving simultaneously to capture everyone named in the indictments.

Arthur is the first one through the door. The others follow him out in a hurry, but they soon get the surprise of a lifetime as all thirty or so officers have their weapons trained on the suspects. "It's over! Drop your weapons and get on the ground!" Bruce Carmen, the FBI chiefs voice bellows over a megaphone.

Arthur or Christopher immediately drops to his knees and surrenders his weapon. Jules follows along, and within minutes the mobsters are in police custody.

TAKE DOWN

At the Parello home, the mob boss Vincent Parello along with several other top mob officials are captured by surprise. Drunk and disorderly the rowdy gangsters tries to fight back, but they are over matched by the number of federal agents. It is the largest bust of an organized crime outfit ever in the United States Federal Bureau of Investigation's history.

"Transport for the prisoners have arrived, sir." An officer tells Bruce Carmen. Bruce watches as agents chain and hood each of the four prisoners, a big grin on his smug face.

The officers load the captured mobsters onto a modified paddywagon, one by one. Just before Arthur is put onto the truck, he is led off to the side and into a separate holding vehicle.

Inside Arthur's cuffs and hood are removed by one of the two FBI agents that he 'shot' inside the compound. "Hey Ron! Gil! I'm glad you guys are okay." Arthur says to the pair sitting across from him in the enclosed van. "You guys really sold that shooting. Man, I was so worried they would get a shot off with that machine gun before you guys could get to the ground."

"Art, you were great. Congratulations! I'm sure their will be a vacation or a fat raise waiting for you." Ron Leonard tells him as the van they are riding in takes a different path than the Black Maria ahead of them.

13.

Some of the criminals captured at secondary locations were already arriving at the booking outpost. Their mugshots are taken, and fingerprints recorded. The mobster associates are stripped and checked for weapons and objects, and issued their new wardrobe. A brand new orange jumpsuit.

Federal investigators are already dragging the prisoners into the interrogation room. Many of the mobsters truly were loyal to the bone, but there usually is a few bottom feeders that will turn on the bosses to cop out for a plea deal on a lesser charge.

Arthur Santiago's van arrives at the local FBI Field office. He is ushered inside without cuffs, and arrives to cheer and applause from fellow field officers, local authorities, and close friends. Bruce Carmen is at the tail end of the line of handshakes that lead to his office.

Finally Arthur and Bruce are left alone and enter Bruce's office to talk. Arthur sits down across from Bruce's desk. Bruce sat on top of his desk facing Arthur.

TAKE DOWN

"You did a great job Art. I'm really proud of you." Bruce tells his friend. "I know your probably still a little upset with me, but I want you to know that how ever much time you need off. It's yours. And if there is anything else."

Arthur just looks at him. "No. There's nothing else. I just want to be left alone for a while."

"No problem. But you know your going to be known as a hero now." Bruce tells him, as he moves the mouse on his computer desk. He looks at the computer screen. "We have apprehended thirty out of thirty-six on that indictment you got us. That's pretty amazing." Bruce just sits there for a moment.

There is a long pause. "Are we done here?" Arthur asks his boss. "I'm tired and hungry, and I want to go home." He stands up and turns for the door. "You have the Parello's and the paintings are safe and sound." Arthur hands Bruce the chrome cannister, containing the paintings.

"If you need to talk to someone... To let out about what you saw." Bruce offers his longtime friend.

Arthur turns for the exit. "Maybe, I'll write a book." Arthur tells him.

"Alright, Art. Keep in touch. Again, great work man." Bruce tells Arthur as he opens the door and leaves Bruce's sight for the last time.

14.

Less than an hour later, just outside of town near McCarran International Airport, Art sits at the counter inside a diner. He just finished eating and hands the waitress a ten dollar bill. "Keep the change." Arthur tells her as he gathers his belongings. He sees his picture on the television. It's a news report on the mob bust. Arthur knows it's time to go. If anyone in or around the mob that wasn't picked up notices him, he'll be the next victim of murder.

He walks out the door and to the curb where his Mercedes Benz CLK 550 is parked. He opens the trunk and slides a manila file folder into one of the two large pieces of luggage.

Arthur hops in the drivers seat and starts the car up. He inputs his GPS for the airport, but then decides to turn his GPS unit off all together. Arthur puts the car in drive and peels out and speeds off down the street. He has one last pick up before heading to the airport.

15.

SIX HOURS LATER

Bruce Carmen is stretched out with his feet on his desk. He leans back in his chair, his hands behind his head.

Bruce is startled as Agent Winters knocks, then quickly opens the door and enters. "Sir, we analyzed the paintings that you gave us earlier." Winters told his boss.

"And?" Bruce snaps, aggravated by the interruption. He sat forward in his chair, with a cold demeanor.

Winters takes a step closer. "The paintings aren't real." He says without explanation.

Bruce jumps to his feet. "WHAT?" Bruce shouts. "Are you sure? There has to be a mistake." He isn't sure how to explain it.

"There's no mistake. The real paintings are missing, and the casino manager also is reporting over twelve million dollars stolen from the secondary vault, around the same time." Agent Winters turns to leave his boss alone.

Bruce slams his hand against the wooden desk. "Winters! Wait! Assemble a team, and locate Agent Arthur Santiago for questioning."

"Yes, sir." Winters disappears from the office leaving Bruce Carmen to clutch his desk and grind his teeth in anger.

After steaming for a few minutes Bruce finally picks up his office phone. He knows it's a long shot, but dials Arthur Santiago's cell phone number anyway.

16.

Arthur is waiting on his luggage after his long international flight. He yawns and stretches, then sees his two piece checked luggage come around the conveyor belt. Just as he picks up the last piece of luggage his cell phone rings. Arthur rolls his belongings out of the airport as he glances at the incoming number on his cell. Arthur just turns the power on the phone off and tosses it in the garbage. He hails a nearby idling taxi, tosses his things in the trunk, then hops inside the backseat.

Inside the taxi he pulls out the manila file folder and looks over the papers inside. It's a transaction receipt to an account owned by a Christopher L. Holt. It is a confirmation of a deposit for $12.6 million. Arthur gives a giant grin to the world as he sits back in the seat and finally is able to breathe easy.

The End.